T0105652

Books by Marshall Frank:

Beyond The Call

Dire Straits

Call Me Mommy

On My Father's Grave

The Latent

Frankly Speaking

Militant Islam in America

From Violins To Violence

Criminal InJustice in America

Messages

Short Stories For The Thoughtful

MARSHALL FRANK

authorHOUSE®

AuthorHouse™
1663 Liberty Drive
Bloomington, IN 47403
www.authorhouse.com
Phone: 1-800-839-8640

First published by AuthorHouse 4/22/2011

ISBN: 978-1-4567-6315-2 (e)
ISBN: 978-1-4567-5971-1 (sc)

Library of Congress Control Number: 2011906318

Printed in the United States of America

Table of Contents

Preface

Spare time creates a precarious lull in the life of a compulsive writer. It usually means that something — anything — must be cranked out or else a spouse, friends, neighbors or kids will suffer from a deluge of unwanted attention. Ergo, books, letters, political op-eds, e-mails and short stories.

Like most authors will attest, writing is like an addiction, not much different from cigarettes, drugs, gambling or sex. You get hooked after the first feel-good experience, then spend the rest of your life trying to duplicate the same feeling. However, by writing you can create a finished product, not get finished by a product you don't create. Why else do successful authors, amid all their wealth and prosperity, continue to lock themselves in a room for months at a time to keep pumping out written words by the millions?

Having retired after thirty years in Miami as a patrol cop, homicide detective and then a few command positions, I left with an immense reservoir of stories ready for the keyboard. One lifetime is not enough to capture them all in manuscripts. Add in, the trials and tribulations of multiple marriages, fathering four children, adopting three more and struggles through my own array of addictions and demons until, one day, the storm calmed and the opportunity for creation was at my doorstep. The volume of stories to tell is beyond infinite.

I turned to a life of writing, not only for enjoyment and perhaps a little income, but as a catharsis in which I could express and share the many aspects I've learned from living the good life, the bad life and the sad life. Now it is a blessing to be able to wake up every day with umpteen hours at my disposal, to do what I want to do, not what I have to do.

My first short fiction story emerged sometime in the late 1990s and was readily tucked away. It started as an idea for a book, but I saw that the message could be tightly bound in a far fewer word count. Since then, I've produced another seventeen stories and kept them packaged away for a rainy day. Many of them could have been the basis for a full blown novel.

The rainy day has arrived and it is time to unleash them from the hard drive and publish the collection as a book before the passage of time rendered half of them out-dated.

These are not traditional "war stories" about cops and robbers; rather they chronicle a myriad of emotions gleaned from life and human experience in its most vulnerable states. After all, police officers are humans too. They are about loss, tragedy, struggle, youth, old age, the gift of love, the denial of love and a sprinkle of humor thrown in.

All of these eighteen stories — to a greater or lesser degree — are based on true happenings which I am intimately familiar with or have credible knowledge about. Naturally, I have taken literary license to skew, embellish, exaggerate and add a bit of drama to the text. Some readers may wonder which of them are closest to the truth, so I have provided a measuring device called: "Truth-o-meter." On the title page of each story, readers will see a percentage rating which tells what degree of truth the tale was derived from. But have no doubt, these stories are all fiction with fictional characters, although I suspect some readers will think a particular character is him or her.

Stories should not only entertain, but stimulate thought. Some of the material is dark, some light, some ironic and some frivolous and silly. But there exists a message in each which I hope will be of value to some, or at least, a few. At age seventy-two, all I can offer my fellow human beings is the benefit of vast experience in dealing with emotional trauma and whatever wisdom was gleaned during the course of one man's life.

The messages abound, depending on how one relates them to their own unique lives. Most are clear, some not so clear, but they are there. I hope readers will appreciate them all for their intended purpose: Understanding mankind.

Enjoy.

Love Scene

"Love is, or it ain't. Thin love ain't love at all."
— Toni Morrison

Arnold Rudd was born of humble means in Durham, North Carolina, with a condition later to be known as Attention Deficit Disorder. That term had not yet been invented in 1927, so the boy grew up with adults nagging him to follow rules, settle down, do as he's told, pay attention and shut up! "Lord," his mother often said. "What am I going to do with that kid?"

But Arnold also had talents. Like many borderline Autistics, he could play classical music by ear and write essays without anyone ever teaching him how. But friends were hard to come by because, well, he was so weird. Adults nicknamed him "Harpo" because he had naturally bushy blond hair.

Raised by a widowed mom with burdens of job, home and making ends meet, Arnold spent a lot of time alone in his room with his 78 rpm record player, conducting Beethoven symphonies, singing along with Bing, practicing violin and writing, writing and...writing. His paper and pencil became the outlet for releasing his inner most feelings. Without that natural gift, he might have gone mad. Unless it was a school project, everything he wrote found its way to the circular file.

He managed good grades in English simply because he

could scratch out a book report without ever reading the book. In one tenth grade assignment, students were required to study a major topic for an entire semester, then submit a lengthy report with bibliography and footnotes. It counted for one-half of the semester grade. But, Arnold never studied anything. He waited until the night before the due date and worked eight frenzied hours penning a twenty-nine page report on the history of classical composers — from his head. He fabricated the titles of five books and their authors for a bibliography, and added bogus footnotes in the hopes the teacher would not check them out. She didn't. He got an A Plus.

During the war years, Arnold and his mother moved to Florida where she could find work as a domestic. Known as the campus nerd, the boy ultimately survived his high school years though many of the girls seemed attracted to his intellect. Young adulthood led him to various jobs playing piano in night clubs and violin in local symphony orchestras. Now a handsome twenty-something, girls were drawn to him like moths to the flame, especially when he played strains of a Gypsy Czardas on the violin.

Into his late forties, Arnold had accumulated three wives, three divorces and two children, both raised by their mothers and stepfathers. Young women thought he was a celebrity of sorts and reveled in being associated with a near-genius. He had loved each, but after a short time, they couldn't deal with his oddball ways. Each time he uttered the marriage vows, he truly thought he had found his soul mate, the woman of his dreams. As the relationships fell apart, he valiantly tried to stick through them, "for better or for worse." But, the marriages failed mainly because, well, Arnold was still a weirdo. They all had the same reasons: Distant. Reclusive. Inattentive.

Often, he was found writing — always writing — on paper, on walls, on napkins, on his hands and arms. He could never seem to meet expectations. The women needed more attention. When his wives felt neglected, he felt smothered. He searched for space. He needed freedom to unbridle his mind.

No matter his domestic storms, the addiction to writing never waned. Nearing his fifties, he still looked for quiet, remote corners where he could pour his thoughts, worries, ambitions and fantasies onto paper. Yet, Arnold still craved the elusive quest: Love.

Paula Santiago came from Bogota, Colombia, but had lived in Miami for most of her forty-four years. Arnold met her at a Calle Ocho Festival where she sold her clay sculptures from a ten-foot square tent. Something in those Spanish eyes set her apart from any woman he'd ever known. Close, yet distant. Welcoming, yet independent. Her accent fascinated him. She had boundless energy, an incredible smile and — she had great legs.

Paula had been single for five years, a widow who had survived a bad marriage in the interest of religious faith. Her husband had tested three times the drunkenness limit when he was killed in a car wreck. Her two sons had long moved on. Arnold could see that her passion for art was all-consuming. It defined her.

Paula also thrived on being true to herself. "What you see is what you get," she told him as they embarked on a cautious dating spree. She marveled at his stories and letters and she loved his violin. Her favorite was Ave Maria. *Play it for me, Arnold.* They warned each other not to get serious because, well, they just weren't meant for marriage. After a year of dating, they finally argued. A stupid argument, but one that lit the caution light. It scared the hell out of them, so reminiscent of past loves. Ah, relationships. They never last. The two lovebirds broke up, but ever so reluctantly.

Usually such separations gave Arnold a sense of relief.

This time it was different. He missed Paula desperately. He dreamed of her loving touch, her strength and her devotion. He had been drawn to her own well of solitude and to her immersion into world of art. It reminded him so much, of him.

Two miserable weeks went by. Alone, he reminisced about her soft voice, her comforting words, that incredible feel of an artist's hands and the freedom she gave him. *"It's okay, Arnold, I have a statuette to make, we'll meet at dinner, then cuddle in front of the TV, like always. Go write your stories, your articles, or your diary. Better yet, why don't you write a book?"*

He finally realized what made her irreplaceable. She didn't want him for herself, she wanted him, for himself. She derived pleasure from seeing him bathe in his own achievements. Likewise, she had taught him to enjoy her own immersion in the world of creation. Surely, he had found the woman of his dreams. And surely, she had found the man of her dreams.

Love abounded. Arnold wasn't a weirdo any more. He was okay, just the way he was born.

In the next thirty-five years, Arnold wrote hundreds of published articles and more than twenty books, one of which was nominated for a Pulitzer Prize for fiction. Paula's celebrated art works were constantly on demand and shown at the finest galleries throughout America. Though they enjoyed material riches, their true wealth came from the ceaseless freedom of expression and the joy it gave others.

Her words echoed in his mind and heart. *Remember, Arnold. It is often said, true love consists not in gazing at each other, but looking in the same direction, together.*

As old age arrived, rheumatoid arthritis took control of Paula's body, wracking her with pain in her hands, arms and legs. Finally she had to discontinue art work, unable to use the tools nature gave her to fulfill her the mission. As the arthritic pain intensified, prescriptions were the only source of relief. Yet, she continued to sell her creations.

But Paula was still able to drive, and drive she did. One fall day in 2009, she was driving from a Miami art showing on her way home to Fort Lauderdale. Somehow, she ended up in Homestead, forty miles in the wrong direction. It wasn't the first sign of that dreaded disease. For weeks, Arnold had noticed that she often lost her thought process in mid-sentence, wore only her bra and panties walking out the door, put her socks in the freezer and broke out crying without reason.

Now into his early eighties, Arnold knew his life would become a void without his treasured Paula. He wrote voraciously, excoriating God for doing this to the most wonderful woman on planet Earth. Surely, as she slipped away, he would slip back to being a weirdo again.

During her most lucid moments, he talked with Paula about her disease, and where it was leading the both of them. Dangers lurked, for she was sure to harm herself without professional care. One day, she asked him to put her in a home. "They'll take good care of me there, Arnold, and you'll be fine. You can still write your heart out."

And so he did.

My darling Paula.

We have been in love for 35 years, but in truth, I have loved you all my life. When I first married Barbara, it was you I was pledging my undying love to. When I married Betty and Emma, it was you standing there at the altar when I gave my heart, for better or for worse, til death do us part.

Finally, the real you showed up in 1975. You were so worth waiting for. I'm glad all those relationships failed, for without them, there would never have been a you and me. And I don't think I'd be sitting here today, alive, if you and me had never happened.

You haven't just been the woman of my dreams, you have been the breath of life within me, you've been my path, my reason to live, my wholeness. I love you with all the devotion any human being can bestow. You'll never die, so long as I am alive.

Now we face a new challenge. Fear not, my love. I will always be where you are going, to hold your hand, to cuddle before the TV, and listen to your breath whisper anything ... anything in my ear, for there is nothing you can say that is unworthy.

For these 35 years, we reveled in holding the reins of our own destiny. And, so, we shall remain in charge of our own destiny. Come with me. Be with me. It can't get any better than this. We are so lucky.

Forever, Arnold

Arnold called her adult sons to share a celebration for Paula's seventy-ninth birthday at the Rolling Hills Senior Center in Pembroke Pines, Florida. Despite her mangled body, twisted from arthritis, it was a happy time. Paula could still remember her son's names and soak in their love and appreciation. They sat in her private room with the TV on for background music, all sharing a glass of wine with crackers and cheese. Later, the men hugged their mother goodbye and walked off down the hall, eyes glassy, noses to hankies.

When a replay of *The Golden Girls* had finished showing, Arnold smiled and turned off the TV. The room became quiet. They were alone. Arnold raised his wine glass in a gesture of triumph, quoting Professor Higgins from *My Fair Lady*, "By George, we did it! We lived the dream, my dear

Paula." The sickly woman reached for her wine as well, but instead, he presented her a water glass. "Here, my love."

Arnold's heart welled with sadness and with joy. With a long breath and puffed cheeks, he smiled to ease the moment. Yet, he couldn't control the stream that burst from his eyes. Neither could she. Their eyes locked, lips quivering, followed by soft smiles and a warm, tender kiss.

"I love you so, so much," they whispered to each other without parting their lips.

"Don't be afraid," she told him, stroking his hair.

Arnold poured several tablets from a vial into his hand, which they divided. He turned on a tape recording of himself playing Schubert's *Ave Maria*, then cuddled on the bed in a spooning position, his arm wrapped over her body, hand on her breast and her hand upon his. Arnold never felt more content. He had saved her and himself from an empty hole with no bottom. They'd never be apart.

"Good night, my love."

"Good night..."

Twenty minutes later, a staff attendant found them in a lasting embrace.

On the table, Arnold had penned his last note:
Behold, a love scene.

A Cop's Toughest Job

Grief fills the room up of my absent child, lies
in his bed, walks up and down with me, puts
on his pretty looks, repeats his words.
— William Shakespeare

Buck Wooldridge and C. J. Willis stood at the bank of the man-made rock pit, wiped their brows with sweat-soaked handkerchiefs and waited for police divers to bring the body to shore. At high noon, the July sun baked the southern suburbs of Miami-Dade County, Florida, into a megalopolis of steamed roadways and sweltering humanity. A small gathering of children and neighbors stood behind yellow barrier tape to look on. Only the squawk of police radios disturbed the silence of the moment.

Buck was familiar with Miller Lake. It was his tenth visit here since being assigned to the Homicide Bureau five years before. To C.J. it was all new. As Buck's rookie detective, he had a lot to learn. With all the interviews, sketches and photos taken, it was time to examine the body. They would have no doubts. There was no foul play. Miller Lake had claimed another drowning victim.

The pathetic, limp body of a shaggy haired, eight-year-old boy lay on the shore as his playmates stood beyond the tape, staring. They said his name was Rolando. When the boy had stood up in an aluminum canoe, it suddenly tipped over. He couldn't hold on. Two of his friends could swim. He could not.

The examination would not take long. All the indicators were there, the foaming from the mouth, the fingernail imprints into the palms of his hands, the goose flesh and the dull gaze from lifeless eyes.

After twelve years on the job and three of probing every kind of death scene, Buck was calloused all right, but not so much that he would not feel a lump in his throat each time he was compelled to touch a deceased child. He never failed to think about his own baby sister who plunged into the abyss of Flushing Bay in New York City thirty years earlier, slipping off a slimy log, unable to swim. He would reflect, recall the specific date and think, *Patty would have been thirty-six now.*

C.J., fresh out of uniform, had left his mark as one of the brightest, most aggressive young black officers on the department. The scourge of death and violence had been a natural environment for the twenty-eight year old who grew up in the steamy, drug-riddled milieu of Liberty City. Now a cop for half a decade, he'd seen it all. Rarely a day went by that he was not wading through a hospital emergency room talking to blood spattered nurses and doctors frantically working to save the life of a gunshot victim. Often, he had to deal with the hysteria of families stricken by the curse of inner city crime. Shootings, bodies, blood, he took it all in stride. Part of the job. But dead kids? Well, they were something else.

The heat and the mood would leave a toll on Buck Wooldridge and C.J. Willis this day. The investigation was complete and the boy was on the way to the morgue, but the worst was yet to come. C.J. followed Buck back to the car where they soaked up the air conditioning and started their reports. The dispatcher came on asking if they were ready to take on another case. C.J. reached but Buck picked up the radio.

"That's negative," replied the tall, balding detective. "We are not yet clear for calls."

C.J. looked to his mentor quizzically. "I thought we were finished here. What's up?"

"Finished? Afraid not. You know better than that."

Buck shifted into drive as C.J. swallowed hard and turned his head to watch the traffic pass. Buck understood how C.J. was feeling, but there was no choice. No doubt, C.J. was hoping someone else could do it. Anyone else.

"Is this your first DOA involving a kid?" asked Buck.

"Yeah, since coming to Homicide."

"Brace yourself. This won't be pleasant."

"Why don't we just use the phone and call the house?"

Buck recoiled. "Listen to me, kid. Never. Never make a notification on the phone. You understand? Never."

"Yeah."

Twenty minutes passed before they arrived at their destination. Gravel rocks crunched under the wheels as they pulled in front of the coral pink, one-story apartment building in the Little Havana district of Miami. It wasn't far from the beats and sounds of Calle Ocho, known forty years before as simply; Southwest Eighth Street.

Olive-skinned kids with dirty faces frolicked about in bare feet while they glanced curiously at the two conspicuous men wearing polyester suits; One, a young African-American and the other a pink-faced Irishman sauntered through the Hispanic populated courtyard. C.J. stayed close as Buck meandered to the row of mail boxes in the courtyard where he spotted the name "Arguello" scribbled in pencil under unit number eight. Beads of perspiration formed on Buck's temples. The trek to the end apartment felt like walking the last mile on death row.

The sounds of lively salsa music blared from inside and the aroma of baked chicken and yellow rice stimulated their salivary glands. Buck looked over to his partner who seemed nervous, peering off into the distance at nothing in particular.

"Hope she speaks English," said Buck under his breath. The he looked at his young partner again. "You okay, C.J.?"

"Yeah, man. Let's just get this over with."

Buck sucked a deep breath, hesitated, then knocked. No answer. He knocked harder this time, with the gold ring on his finger. Almost immediately, the volume subsided and footsteps approached the door. A rush of blood swelled in Buck's head as his heart began to pound. Then he gave C.J. a supportive pat on the shoulder. The jalousie window cranked open and a woman asked, "Yes, may I help you?" They were struck by her dark eyes and flawless skin. Petite, no more than thirty, she wore wide rimmed glasses and had full, bright red lips that formed an infectious smile. So trusting. So unsuspecting.

"My name is Sergeant Wooldridge. This is Detective Willis. May we please come in?" He held a gold shield to the screen. It was difficult looking directly in her eyes.

Still smiling, Mrs. Carmen Arguello hurriedly opened her door saying she had to attend to her oven. "I'll be right with you. Please sit."

Seconds seemed like hours. Buck and C.J. sat nervously fiddling with pens, wiping brows, not saying a word. Oppressive heat in the austere apartment made it difficult to breathe. An oscillating fan on the terrazzo floor gave movement to drawn window curtains while a meager ray of sunlight beamed through the glass jalousie door. A portrait of Jesus hung on the wall and an arrangement of framed photographs were set in layered rows upon end tables, mostly of a smiling, laughing, shaggy haired, eight-year old boy.

Finally, clutching a dish towel, the lady emerged. "Please excuse the mess. I am making supper for the little one and myself. Yes, how can I help you?" Her eyes opened wide.

Buck would rather have stuck pins in his eyeballs than to endure this moment. But there was no turning back. A million thoughts raced through his head as the woman stood waiting with her curious, innocent smile. It reminded him of his mother's smile. C.J. stood behind as Buck took the lead.

"Is there anyone here with you, Ma'am?"

Her eyes wrinkled at the center. "No, I am a widow. What is it, please?"

"You have a little boy named Rolando?"

"Yes." She nodded. "Oh dear. What has he gotten in to now?" The broad smile vanished. Her expression changed to exasperation, impatience. Buck and CJ. Looked at each other. "Has he been throwing rocks again?"

There was only one way to do this. Buck stood, swallowed and made hard eye contact. "I'm afraid there's been an accident, Ma'am."

She looked confused, speechless. C.J. looked away. The blank stare in Buck's face told the story. A bowling ball weighed deep in his stomach as perspiration rolled from his brow. Two words. "We're sorry."

As though a blunt instrument struck her from behind, her face compressed into crevices, wrinkles and twisted distortions. First, it was disbelief. No tears. Not yet. Her jaw protruded outward baring teeth while she choked, grabbed her chest and staggered away. Then came the wailing and the pathetic sobbing and then the anger. Alone with this woman they had never known, Buck Wooldridge and C. J. Willis spent the next hour allowing her beat on their chests screaming in a language they did not understand. Yet they knew every word as they held her and comforted her and tried to explain the unexplainable. Buck's eyes welled up.

They always did. C.J. held the woman around the shoulders as she began to collapse.

Before the end of that torturous hour, three human beings of disparate cultures and different tongues had shared a moment that would be etched in their hearts for a lifetime. Buck steeled himself as best he could, braving the depth of emotions while in her presence. But the childhood images of his own mother answering that cold-hearted phone call thirty years before finally whittled him down to a member of humanity. He broke into tears the moment he sat back in his car. C.J. held back, looking away, hanging on to be strong.

Carmen Arguello remained with neighbors and relatives who would see her through the abyss and help ease the shock from such an irretrievable loss.

Buck looked at his watch as C.J. waited, gathering himself thinking about the perils inherent in his job, the crime, the riots, drugs, weaponry, the incessant tidal wave of violence that constantly demanded the need for their existence. It is all dangerous. But he would gladly face a thousand thieves or plunge into the bowels of any street riot rather than face one more Carmen Arguello.

With three hours of duty time to go, he picked up the radio to check in. The dispatcher advised they were backed up with calls and no one else was available to handle a report of child abuse. The victim was at the morgue.

"We're on the way."

Step to the Rear

"You gotta love livin', baby, cause dyin' is a pain in the ass."
— Frank Sinatra

In a vicarious kind of way, people are either fascinated or obsessed with the aft segment of the human body that is otherwise displeasing and associated with horrid odors and filthy emissions. Yet, the all-encompassing adjective is among the most used in American lexicon. Nary a soul has escaped one reference or another to a horse's ass, a pain-in-the-ass, ass-kisser, dumb-ass, big-ass, hard-ass, jackass, fat-ass and just plain "asshole."

Hubert Gantwell was one of those souls. He often found the human posterior be a source of great consternation or at times — depending on the scenario — admiration.

A bus driver for Miami's Transit System for thirty-three years, Hubert worked hard, raised three kids, put one through college, and remained forever faithful to Luanda, the woman he married when they were just old enough to vote. A true Virgo, neat as a pin, meticulous and well-organized, Hubert always kept a tube of sanitizing cream on hand as an essential item in his equipment bag.

Though happily married, Hubert had an eye for the ladies, always flirting and chatting with attractive passengers of the opposite gender, gawking at their fine derrieres through the rear view mirror after they deposited coins in the slot. Sometimes, just before sitting, a lady would turn and catch his admiring eyes in that mirror. Their expressions never wavered: *I caught you looking at my butt.* He'd smile, nod, and pull off into traffic until the next stop, and the next butt.

Colon cancer killed his father at the age of sixty-one. That's why Hubert's doctor insisted that he start getting his colon checked at least every five years, starting at age fifty-five. "Must I?" he asked.

"You must."

"How do you do that?"

The crusty old doctor sensed a good humored fellow in Hubert, so he told it like it was. "Hubert, just like Roto-rooter, we take this long snake with an eye-camera at the end, insert it through your sphincter and ram it through a football field length of intestines looking for polyps or signs of cancer."

Aye yi yi! Hubert broke into a cold sweat. "Can't you just X-ray my bowels?"

"Hubert, it's the Roto-Rooter or nothing."

"I hate when people mess with my, you know..."

"I also hate messing with your 'you-know' Hubert, that's why I'm sending you to a specialist."

"You have specialists, just for that?"

Two weeks later, accompanied by loving Luanda, Hubert showed up at the office of Doctor Dale P. Burnside. The scene was already building in his head, wondering how his anus would be manipulated, penetrated and abused by another human being. Worse, how would it look? He hadn't had a drink in fifteen years, thanks to Alcoholics Anonymous. But this might be the proverbial straw.

Luanda had calmed him as they waited for Doctor Burnside to enter the room. "Don't worry so much, sweetie. People go through this all the time."

The door opened. The nurse looked bedraggled, hair pinned in a sloppy pony tail, attractive but impersonal. "Hello, Mr. Gantwell," she said, checking her file folder.

"Uh, hello, Ma'am. When is the doctor coming?"

She turned and glared at poor Hubert. "Mr. Gantwell. I *am* your doctor. I *am* a gastro-enterologist"

Hubert's jaw nearly hit the floor. Speechless now, visions of this woman breaching his sphincter danced in his head. The shock must have shown in his eyes while the doctor smirked, "Don't worry, Mr. Gantwell. I've done this five thousand times."

This woman has penetrated five thousand assholes? Why would anyone going to medical school choose assholes for a specialty?

Days felt like years as he pondered the appointment for his first colonoscopy. He had never even seen his own sphincter, now some strange woman was about to go where no one had ever been before. What did it look like? Did some sphincters look nicer than other sphincters?

In the privacy of his bedroom, while Luanda was out shopping, Hubert took a face mirror and bent over like a contortionist trying to get a view of that forbidden zone. *Ugh! You gotta be kidding me.*

Thoughts raged, thoughts which he dared not discuss with Luanda. *Powder? Make-up? Lipstick?* Then he eased up. *I know, I'll use a magic marker and write, "Come in. Welcome!"* Oh well. The exercise elevated his mood as Hubert laughed out loud.

Luanda tried her best to sooth his nerves, but he seemed to fall apart at the mere concept of the invasive procedure. Twelve hours ahead of A-Day, he drank the God-awful solution, then found himself glued to the toilet seat for two hours, cleansing himself for the good lady doc.

The day of reckoning arrived. Hubert was shaking like a

vibrator as Luanda held him by the arm entering the clinic. "Right this way, Mr. Gantwell," said a receptionist.

Oh God, that woman knows why I'm here. Why is she smiling?

Hubert was led to a bed enclosed only by thin hospital drapery, one of many in a row of beds. Other "victims" were stationed on each side of him. When Luanda helped him tie the hospital gown in the rear, she gave Hubert a little pinch.

"Ahhhh" he screamed suddenly. "Luanda! Why did you...?"

Luanda chuckled. Hubert frowned.

A nurse arrived. "Is everything all right, Sir?"

Hubert looked to his wife, "Luanda, why are you laughing. That wasn't funny."

Doctor Burnside came in to soothe the frightened patient. She explained that he would be given a short-term anesthetic and assured him everything would be all right.

"Can we just get this over with?"

Suddenly, a nearby patient released a flatulent emission of booming dimensions. It sounded like a roaring motorcycle blasting away for several seconds. Hubert figured it must have set a duration record, one for the famed Guinness Book.

The moment of reckoning arrived. Hubert was wheeled into the operating room and there she was, petite and disheveled. Smiling and wearing goggles, Doctor Burnside was ready to invade his most private of sanctuaries. Then, a face mask lowered onto his ... zzzzzzzzzzzz.

It seemed that mere seconds had passed when he awakened inside one of those cloth-draped cubicles, barely four feet from other patients on either side. Luanda greeted him, smiled and held his hand. The moment she leaned over to kiss him, a nurse approached his bed. That's when his blow-hole exploded so abruptly that Luanda leaped a foot off the floor and the nurse spun an about-face. Hubert shrugged, then chuckled. "Did you hear what that asshole said?"

A woman in the next bed howled with laughter. Then, a fellow on the other side, "Har Har Har." A chorus of howling roared throughout the room. Luanda doubled over, "My stomach, my stomach," she screamed.

Hubert's record-splitting fart was a moment for the ages.

All's well that ends well. Hubert was cancer free and he would not have to endure another backside invasion for another five years.

But it sure changed the way he viewed women's posteriors in that rear view mirror.

Engines of the Heart

"The mass of men lead lives of quiet desperation"
— Henry David Thoreau

Dedicated. Obsessed. Sharp.

Those words best described Swain Dougherty, Miami-Dade homicide detective extraordinaire. If he didn't need the money, he would have worked for nothing. Every day, Detective Dougherty awakened eager to seize another crime scene, track a killer, examine cadavers, conduct interrogations and sort pieces of puzzles together before handing a case over to the prosecutor's office wrapped in a velvet bow, assured of conviction. He relished the witness stand, daring defense lawyers to trip him up, reciting detailed confessions from memory, showing off before the legal community just how "slick" he really was.

But it was destined to fall apart.

When he was eight years-old, his alcoholic mother swallowed fifty sleeping pills and checked into eternal oblivion. That left him to be raised by a gung-ho, San Diego Marine who forced him to do push-ups morning and night, eat at attention, study weaponry and prepare for a military career. Love and affection was for sissies, not *real* men.

He could not call his father "Dad." *SIR, may I go out and play? May I be excused from the table, SIR? Yes SIR! No SIR!*

Swain disappointed *SIR* because he was slightly built. He desperately tried to please *SIR*, but he just could not do all those pull-ups or scale the rigorous obstacles courses. To *SIR's* chagrin, Swain took no real interest in guns.

He often thought about his mother, recalling the whisper in her voice and those loving eyes. Swain missed her terribly, but dared not utter his feelings aloud.

He met sixteen year-old Tamika in his eleventh grade class, a petite Japanese-American girl with whom he fell deeply in love. She had velvet gold skin, long black satin hair and brown eyes slanted over her cheekbones. Daily, they embarked on clandestine trysts at her house when her parents were not at home.

SIR would have none of it, his son consorting with another race. *SIR* scuttled the relationship and arranged a transfer to another base in North Carolina.

The two lovers wrote secret letters promising to be true, awaiting the day when they would be together once more. Day and night, Swain fantasized her touch, her eyes, her soft, sweet breath.

Suddenly, the letters stopped coming. He wrote to her again and again. No response. Six months later, Swain took off in search of Tamika, only to arrive in California a day after her wedding. She was five months pregnant. Too late.

Depression ravaged his soul. He wandered in anonymity to remote places in Iowa and Missouri where he experimented with drugs and worked menial jobs. For once, he had not a care in the world, no *SIR*, no screaming in the morning. *Against the bulkhead boy... you're nothing but a loser!*

At nineteen, knowing it would infuriate his father, he joined the United States Army. "You little piece of crap," Sir shouted on the phone. "This was a Marine Corps family. Now, YOU!"

Thin and gangly, Swain gained self-confidence during

his four years of military service. Though he dated now and then, no woman could ever replace Tamika.

During the six years after leaving the Army, Swain drifted from city to city where he lived in cheap rooms searching for a niche. He found good jobs operating heavy construction equipment before ending up in Miami, Florida. That's where he met Arnie Mirkovich.

One mid-June afternoon, Swain heard three gunshots from behind a shopping plaza. He saw two young Latino men run to a waiting pick-up truck. An older, heavy-set man lay motionless on the pavement. As the truck squealed away, an hysterical woman tended to the fallen one. Curious, Swain followed the truck keeping it in sight for four miles until the vehicle backed into the driveway of an old duplex. Swain used his cell phone to call police. They arrived within minutes.

"I'm Detective Sergeant Mirkovich," announced the cop, flashing a gold shield.

"Hi. My name's Swain Dougherty. I saw those guys shoot someone behind a shopping plaza, about four miles from here."

Minutes later, the two killers were hauled out in handcuffs. "We could never have solved this case without you," Detective Mirkovich said.

WOW!

Later, Arnie Mirkovich invited Swain to join other detectives for lunch at a nearby restaurant. Swain watched and listened, feeling the camaraderie. They weren't just talking about a job, they were talking about a passion. The job was actually something they enjoyed.

"So, what do you do, Mr. Dougherty," asked a female detective.

"Heavy equipment operator."

"Gets kinda hot out there this time of year, doesn't it?"

After lunch, Arnie Mirkovich took him aside. "That

thing you did, Swain. That was real slick. You'd make a great cop. Ever think about wearing the badge?"

The next night, Swain rode as an observer with a uniformed police officer on patrol. Six months later, Swain "Slick" Dougherty graduated number one in his academy class. Now, at thirty years of age, Swain was somebody. *"You're nothing but a loser."* No, Swain was a winner, a cop, a symbol of integrity, admired and respected if only for wearing that uniform and fighting the scourge of crime. Now, folks were calling him *Sir!* "I'm sorry, *Sir!*" "I didn't see that stop sign, *Sir.*" Two years later, as a seasoned cop, he was transferred into Homicide where he would work beside Arnie Mirkovich.

After his training, he met the challenge of murder investigations like a Peyton Manning quarterback spearheading his football team to victory every game. It must have been a gift of nature. In his first year, he left no case unsolved. Amazed at his prowess, prosecutors relished him as a state's witness.

One night, Swain was dispatched to a local bistro featuring topless dancers where a patron had been shot and killed. The jealous husband of a dancer had been arrested for murder by uniformed police on the scene. The woman remained for questioning. With her lover dead and her husband in jail, she was all alone.

She wore red pumps and a man's sport jacket to cover her naked body while she nervously lit a filtered cigarette. A warm chill came over Swain the moment he saw her.

"Your name, Ma'am?"

"Kimberly Wallace."

"I need to ask you some questions."

"Questions? I really don't want to have to testify. Do I have to?"

She was stunningly exotic with long, black satin hair,

Asian eyes, olive skin and a porcelain complexion. Swain hesitated in his questions, absorbed by her beauty. "Why are you looking at me that way?" she asked

"Sorry, Ma'am. You remind me of someone I knew once."

For the next three weeks, he could not erase her from his mind. Swain had found another Tamika.

The next Sunday night, while off duty, Swain visited the cabaret. Kimberly was on stage bumping and grinding to the delight of the male audience. Spotlights followed her every move, altering colors from red to blue, then green. Whistles from the gallery pierced his ears. As he found an empty table, she cupped a hand over her brow to see through the glare. She smiled. He smiled back, waving.

After her dance, Kimberly strutted into the audience and took a chair next to Swain. "Hey, aren't you the detective...?"

"Yes, Ma'am. Uh, I just needed to do a little follow up investigation."

"Oh really? Look, if you think...I'm not a hooker, okay?"

"Oh, no Ma'am. I was just — "

"You want to date me, don't you?" she asked with aplomb.

"No, Ma'am, un..."

"How about Monday night. I'm off. I really like seafood. Then you can ask me all the *official* questions."

The date was filled with laughter and chatter. Swain was amazed that a stripper could be so conversant. She spoke of being the illegitimate child of an American sailor, admitting that her marriage to Sam Wallace had been her ticket to the United States.

"Mind if I ask a sensitive question?" He rattled his ice cubes.

"You want to know why I'm a stripper, right?" She laughed. "I'm from Malaysia. Sam was an aircraft mechanic there. Our family lived in a thatch hut with no drinking water except for the river, and no clothes other than donations. Today, my mother has her own house, a refrigerator, a washing machine, even a television."

"That's great."

She smelled like she had just stepped out of a bubble bath. Swain Doughtery was complete again, fully absorbed in this woman's sheer existence. With the wrap of her fingers behind his neck as they made love, so gentle, so soft, his heart billowed the familiar passion he had felt toward Tamika.

The wedding took place in a judge's chambers the day after her divorce was final. Though he was the butt of jokes for marrying a stripper, it was nothing illegal. Swain took it in stride.

Miami-Dade County was a virtual factory for murder cases. Swain's overtime investigations consumed sixty to ninety hours a week, plus off-duty court appearances which boosted his overtime earnings to six figures a year. They bought two new cars and a large home with a swimming pool. In the beginning, they made love two and three times a day.

Swain solved seven whodunits that year and basked in the plaudits of lawyers, judges and supervisors. He had love, he had respect, he had good health and everything a man could hope for. *"Homicide Detective Swain Dougherty here."*

Out-of-town investigations, high profile cases and endless court commitments created incessant demands. When he'd arrive home and stumble through the door, Swain headed for a cool bed to sleep, nothing else. Kimberly accused him of being more in love with his job than with her.

One morning, over breakfast, she made a demand. "Prove it to me."

"Prove what?"

"You always say that you love me more than anything, including your job. Now it's time to show me."

And, he did. He loved her so.

With great reluctance, Swain surrendered the badge and returned to the steaming interstate highways operating heavy equipment. It paid well, but he missed the special camaraderie and that incredible high of feeling significant, that he made a difference in the world. A year went by and Swain was feeling a huge void in his life. The job was intolerable.

"Haven't I proven my love for you, Kim?" he asked.

"Yes, baby. I must admit, you have. If you want to return to the police department, I'll understand. It's okay."

It was better than ever, high fives, laughter and new challenges as he resumed the comradery with friends like Arnie Mirkovich. At last, Swain was back doing what he did best, wrapping up those cases, tracking killers and handing over velvet-bowed cases to prosecutors. With it all, came the demand for overtime work, his court commitments and the absence from home, again.

Six months passed. It was a stormy Thursday afternoon when Swain came home and noticed the pictures of his Malaysian mother-in-law were missing from atop the bookcase. Kim's clothes were gone from the closet. Near the kitchen sink, he found a note written in blue ink on a yellow pad:

Dear Swain,
I care for you Swain, but I cannot live with you. I promise I will not fight you for anything. I have so much more than what I would have in my country. I cannot complain. I'll be staying at Beverly's house for a while. This is best. Please don't call me. Stay well, Swain. Keep solving those cases.

Love, Kim

As he once lost Tamika, he now had lost Kimberly.

Swain fell into a deep depression which consumed him day and night. For the next three weeks, people at work asked why he seemed in such a fog. He forgot testimony, misplaced evidence and turned onto one-way streets in the wrong direction. Arnie implored him to take time off.

Each time Swain tried calling Kim on the phone, she hung up or refused to answer. She closed her Facebook page and would not respond to his e-mails. He drove past Beverly's house often, but rarely saw her car there. He wondered where she had gone, what she was doing, who she was seeing.

A week later, on a muggy summer Tuesday, Swain arrived at the office feeling drained of energy. "There is a pile of messages in your box," advised the office secretary. "Three prosecutors, some witnesses and some woman who called three times asking for you."

"Was it Kim?"

"No."

"I'll call back later."

He grabbed the county car keys, signed out on the board and said to Arnie, "I'll be on the cell phone. I want to be alone today."

Swain drove to the police union office where he checked his insurance policies. Then he sent a dozen roses to Kimberly with a note attached. The radio dispatcher gave him three messages to call his office. He didn't bother. Instead, he bought a quart of gin at a local liquor store. When he did call the office, the secretary said some woman was still trying to contact him, but it wasn't Kim. "I'll get it later," he replied.

Guzzling straight from the bottle, he drove the unmarked police car to his house in South Miami and left the keys on the car seat. A legal pad lay atop the dining room table, an invitation to pour blood from a broken heart through his pen. He removed half his clothes, lifted the pen and began writing. He drank in gulps while tender images of his mother flashed through his head. Weeping, he asked aloud, "Why, Mom? Why did you have to die?" His tongue caught the salty taste of tears as they dripped upon the note pad, smearing ink as he wrote to his beloved Kimberly.

> *...there is no one on the face of this earth who will love you as I have loved you. But that doesn't matter any more... I never fail to lose everyone I've ever loved...it is my destiny. I will be with you again someday, with Tamika, and my mother and no one, not even God can take that away from me.*

Three-fourths of the bottle was gone in less than an hour. Eyes bleary, he lay the pen down in mid-sentence and called his beloved wife one more time. This time, she answered.

"Swain, please don't..."

"I want you to have ... (hic) ... good life, Kimverly."

"Swain. You're drunk. Where are you?"

"Don't matter, shweetheart...where I'm going...matters."

"Swain, are you at home? Tell me."

"G-night shweetheart...my love...my Kimverly. Until we're together again." He slammed the cell phone into the garbage.

Swain was not aware than Kimberly had called on another phone to the homicide office to alert Arnie Mirkovich about his ominous call. Arnie and a partner jumped in an unmarked police car, lay the blue flasher atop the roof and pressed the accelerator to the floor.

Meanwhile, Swain had always wondered how this would feel. He'd seen it a hundred times, in the aftermath from the perspective of a detective.

He took one more swig from the green bottle, grabbed a framed photo of Kimberly, then staggered into the bedroom.

Her bedroom. He set the photo on the floor at the side of the bed where they had made love so often, then breathed deep to imagine the aroma of her bubble bath scent. "I love you, Kimverly."

He set a dresser mirror on the floor against the wall across from the bed. After one last swig, he sat on the carpet between mirror and bed, gazing at his image, drooling. From under the mattress, he removed his .380 caliber Glock, semi-automatic pistol, stared at himself then glanced toward the photo of him and Kimberly. Looking in the mirror again, he inserted the cold, steel barrel into his mouth...wondering... *Is there any doubt?*

The strident sound of screeching brakes sounded from outside the bedroom window. He heard car doors slam shut. The clock had run out. The time was now. He gazed once more at his mouth slobbering around the muzzle. Then his sight shifted to the photo of Kimberly, impaling the image of her slanted eyes in his brain as the hammer dropped.

Silence.

*

POP!

Just as he rushed outside the car door, Arnie Mirkovich heard the single shot from inside the corner window of the house. Both detectives raced to the house. Arnie knew it was too late. They broke through the rear door and ran through the kitchen where the odor of alcohol pervaded the air. Inside the bedroom, they discovered their friend at peace, slumped forward on the floor between the wall and the bed. Blood and fluids drained from his face. The two beleaguered cops stood in shock, then began sobbing. Arnie screamed aloud, "Why, God?"

Swain Dougherty spent a lifetime pursuing the one goal

he always found elusive. After all, *love* was all he ever really craved. *Love*, the engine of his heart. Three times it was his, three times, it was lost.

No one would ever deny him again.

As Arnie Mirkovich stood over the corpse wiping tears, he dropped a crumpled piece of paper into the pool of blood. On it, was a hand-written message:

Call Tamika. Important. 305-534-9831.

Truth-o-meter: 30%

Christmas Cop

"A hero is one who does what he can. The others don't."
— Romain Rolland

It was to be another ordinary day as Douglas Walter Covington awakened to the morning alarm, his head wracked from too many martinis the night before. Oh, those Christmas Eve parties at the lodge. After a quick shower, he donned a wrinkled uniform, holstered his nine-millimeter, gobbled a banana and headed into the steaming streets of North Miami Beach. That was his beat.

Whoops. Almost forgot.

Once on duty, he raced back to his garage apartment to retrieve Tyrone, the furry Tyrannosaurus Rex with the red satin bow around its neck. He placed it in the rear seat of the cruiser. If time allowed, he'd try to sneak down to Surfside during lunch break.

Winters in Hoboken were a distant childhood memory as the December sunshine baked South Florida like the Sahara in summer. This year, he hoped to visit his little boy during Christmas or, at least, hear his sweet chuckle over a telephone. Douglas was a newcomer to divorced life.

Holidays had been a time of joy and togetherness. He once cherished the early morning excitement of a precious child, the aroma of blue spruce, the sounds of the Mormon

Tabernacle Choir singing *Joy To The World*, eggnog, fruit cake and the touch of a loving woman. Alas, no excitement this year. No eggnog. No hugs. No family.

Not much giving today, only taking. The taking of freedom that is — arresting lawbreakers. His job.

Matthew's photo lay upon the dash. Halfway through his shift, Douglas had already settled a fight between two bar flies, one of whom vomited on his spit-polished shoes. Before that, he locked up a jealous husband while settling a violent domestic. Three burglar alarm calls all proved to be false. A backlogged dispatcher was pressuring the sergeant to hustle his officers from call to call.

Traffic was oddly sparse for a Wednesday morning, a stark reminder to Douglas that this was a special day. Kids everywhere rode shiny new bicycles. One of them, somewhere out there, was his. He thought about the years past, of spectacular family dinners, Sharon's deep blue eyes and silken hair, of ski trips to Beech Mountain and cruises to Cancun. Now, she had a new life without him, remarried, happily. He had regretted his infidelity a thousand times, offered a million apologies, but it could not reverse destiny. The chapter was over. His weakness in the face of opportunity was no excuse. She could not forgive, nor ever trust again. His mind drifted, visualizing her endearing smile.

Suddenly, movement ahead shocked him back to the present.

A late model Nissan was speeding east on the west bound side of the road, weaving, jerking from side to side. Flashers. Siren. An easy ticket. Minutes later, a large bearded black fellow reeking of whiskey staggered beside the police car trying desperately to touch the tip of his nose or walk a line, mumbling like he had a mouthful of wet sponge. The arrest was imminent. No choice.

"Please, Offisher. I gotta see my kids. Please don't put me in jail on Chrishmish day. I'm sorry. I'm really sorry."

Douglas dutifully handcuffed the disheveled man and placed him in the back seat of his patrol car.

"Oh Geez, this is gonna mess up my kids somethin' awful."

"How many kids do you have, Luther?"

"Two. Melinda's nine, Willie's ten. Please, Offisher. I just got divorced. Lost my house, car, everything. My life's ruined." The drunk began sobbing. "I know I was wrong. Please. Gimme a break. I'll lose my job."

Doug lifted the police radio, his mind racing with options. It was time to summon the prisoner transport unit. He pressed the button, then held back, thinking. *Christmas day, two kids, newly divorced.* He turned and watched Luther Tyrone Manning wallow in self pity, listing and swaying, strangely juxtaposed to that lifeless, furry dinosaur sitting beside him. The fellow seemed a decent sort, if he was sober. Computer records showed no past arrests, not even a traffic ticket.

But the sergeant's orders were clear and the department's policy unwavering about drunk drivers. Douglas' job was merely to enforce the law.

He reflected on that late night party at the lodge, his own arduous drive back to the apartment through blurred eyeballs and a spinning head. He shook his head. *Yes. No. Yes. No.* Finally, he keyed the mike and ordered the dispatcher. "Uh, please send a taxi cab to Biscayne Boulevard and Sunny Isles. Stranded motorist here."

Hope the Sarge doesn't find out.

At twelve thirty-five, no calls were holding, a good time to call little Matthew. He grabbed a cup of gratis coffee at a donut house, took out his cell phone, punched seven numbers and imagined the size of that little boy's eyes when he saw that dinosaur. The phone rang four times before the beep, then...Sharon's voice:

"Hello. You have reached 534-9685. Paul, Matthew and I are out of town for the holidays. If you would like to leave your name and number — "

Out of town for the holidays? Oh well.

Thirty minutes later, Douglas was en route to one of those insidious alarm calls when he heard his call number again.

"Are you in the area of Eastern Shores?"

"That's QSL," he answered, "I'm en route to a fifteen."

"Cancel your fifteen."

He lay the mike on the seat and pulled to the roadside to write. From the radio, the sound of a sustained, high pitched beep signaled an emergency call about to be broadcast. The dispatcher's voice was clear as a Christmas bell.

"6241, a forty-one, child drowning..." His pen was out of ink. Nothing to write with. "At 3510 Northeast 171st street." He muttered to himself, *memorize the address and get rolling. No time to lose.* The call was urgent, life threatening. "...small boy fell in a pool..." While she repeated the information, he turned on the overhead flashers, blared the siren and took off like a shot. It was only two miles away.

Cars scrambled to the roadside as he sped easterly across the causeway, siren wailing, beacons flashing. He cut a sharp left on two wheels into a residential district, then a fast right and another left searching for street signs. Four more streets to go. He passed the main artery then backed up, turned left, then right at the next corner. A bustle of activity could be seen in the distance where he sped toward a cul de sac. As he screeched to a stop, a swarm of neighborhood people, mostly women, raced to his police cruiser and pointed frantically toward the graffiti-marked house at the far end. The instant he switched off the siren, the strident shrill of a screaming woman in the distance pierced his eardrums. A large, balding man in a Miami Dolphins tee shirt led the crowd motioning for the officer to hurry. "This way, this way," he shouted. *Pop the trunk, get the emergency kit, go with the crowd. Hurry. Hurry!*

A surge of blood rushed to his head as he followed the intense shriek of the woman's voice, running closer and finally to the rear of the house. She was on her knees inside a dilapidated screened patio, trembling hands folded to her heart facing the green, murky pool water, yelling unintelligible Spanish at the top of her lungs. Her face contorted, arms flailing, she turned to the officer, pleading for help.

More people swarmed the officer, babbling hysterically in foreign tongues demanding his attention. Doug felt a surge of panic. He had to do something now and fast. This was no academy exercise. No Resuscitator Annie here. The world was watching, it seemed, and there was a two-year-old boy somewhere in that pit of thick, green algae water. The house had been abandoned for months.

Mama was a portly woman with dark hair that covered her face like a wet mop. She tore at his uniform, eyes bulging, ranting in a language that the officer did not know, but understood. Her screams were deafening.

In less than ten seconds, the officer shed his gun belt and shoes. "How long has he been in there?" he asked one of the bystanders.

"Less than five minutes," a man's voice shouted back.

Five minutes? Little time left. Hurry.

He dove into the murky water. It was like trying to see through an ocean of vomit. With no field of vision, he squeezed his eyes shut and pumped his way to the floor of the pool where he felt the smoothness of slimy concrete. Like a scavenging catfish, he blindly swam back and forth along the pool bed hoping, praying to feel the flesh of a boy.

Seconds felt like hours. Then, an object! Doug pulled on an old lawn chair, and let it go. His lungs felt ready to explode as he struggled to the surface.

Gasping, he saw anticipation in all their eyes as he broke the plane of the water. Treading water, he shook his head sadly as Mama perched on her hands and knees, screaming relentlessly. The large, bald man threw his hands to his head and turned away. "I'm sorry," choked the officer, "I'll go back. I'll find him." Panting, he treaded water for several seconds then sucked a huge breath before submerging once more, this time to the shallow end. Too much time had passed. The boy could never survive.

Again, like that blind catfish, he traversed the pool bottom, back and forth, groping, feeling, praying. Suddenly, just inches below the surface at the corner stairs, he felt a tiny foot. Then, a leg, a body. *My God, it's him. I've got him.* He pulled the small child to him and emerged from the water, shocking onlookers like a swamp monster. Unnerved by the cacophony of a roaring crowd, he raised the limp child over his head and onto the coping. No time to lose. Spitting, coughing and gasping for breath, the officer asked the bald man to restrain Mama as she raced over.

First, he squeezed the boy's chest, holding him upside down to drain his pipes and lungs. There were no signs of life, no pulse, no breathing. His pupils failed to dilate. *It's too late,* he thought, *the boy is dead.* But they were all watching. He had to try. He had to go through the motions.

Doug Covington had been on the job for only a year and never performed CPR outside a classroom. Frantically, his mind searched the far reaches of his training. "Give me room," he demanded. He felt a sudden chill as the wet uniform clung to his body. Shrouded with the responsibility of preserving a human life, he carefully went to work, patient, determined, just as he was taught. "Back off, please," he pleaded again to the hovering crowd. *Why is that rescue unit taking so long?*

Deep in concentration, he began with short, rhythmic depressions to the boy's breast bone. Then he cupped his lips over the child's nose and mouth and blew short, rapid breaths into his lifeless airways. Onlookers, including Mama, were eerily silent as they watched the officer, some standing, some kneeling, some with hands to their faces, praying. Seconds, minutes passed with no response.

A pall of pessimism chilled the crowd. Mama wailed pleas to God in her native tongue. But Doug kept on, blowing, depressing and blowing again, hoping for that rescue unit. Suddenly, like a bursting bubble, the boy coughed directly into the officer's mouth. He coughed, then choked, and coughed again. Everyone gasped. Mama exploded into tears, unable to utter a sound. Miraculously, the boy's eyes fluttered and color started to return to his purple skin. Then came the sounds of cheering and laughing as the boy sputtered and cried. Exhausted, dazed, Doug hardly felt all the hands slapping his shoulders, pounding on his back.

"Thank you."

"Great job."

"You did it! You did it!"

"Gracias, Senor."

At last, the welcome sound of a siren from the rescue ambulance drew closer, then stopped. Rescue had arrived. With the boy cradled in his arms and the crowd in pursuit, Doug raced to the front of the house. He transferred the wet, confused child to a husky woman wearing an emergency medical technician's uniform. When he took one last look at the boy, the image of his own son flashed through his brain, dark hair, brown eyes, so innocent, so in love with life.

The moment he turned around, Mama leaped upon him with a bear hug; holding and kissing his weary face. She gushed tearful praises in Spanish and English. That was the moment Douglas Walter Covington realized the enormous feat he had just accomplished. He alone had saved the life of a child.

Mama departed inside the ambulance to be with little Rolito. Sopping and exhausted, Doug returned to his patrol car emotionally and physically spent. He paused a few moments to catch his breath then lifted the mike to advise the dispatcher. "I'm clear. The child is QRU. I'll be out of service about forty minutes to change uniforms."

"That's QSL," answered the dispatcher.

He glanced over and saw the crowd looking on from their yards, several women and the large balding fellow who smiled and waved. He buckled up, started the engine and pulled the gear shift into drive when a barefoot girl about ten years old, with long black hair, approached his window. "Merry Christmas," she said with a toothy smile.

Oh yeah. Christmas. "Well, Merry Christmas to you, too," he replied. With a broad smile, and a warm heart, he reached into the back seat, grabbed the furry Tyrannosaurus Rex with the red bow and passed it to the young girl. "Here," he said. "His name is Tyrone. Would you give it to that little boy?"

"Oh yes, sir," she replied, beaming. "And what's your name?"

"Covington. Doug Covington," he answered, gazing down at his son's photograph.

It was a day of giving after all.

Truth-o-meter: 40%

Serendipity at Live Oak

*"There is no duty more obligatory than
the repayment of kindness"*
— Cicero

January, 2011 - Port St. John, Florida

Gigi Tennison stood from her wheel chair and struggled to blow out the small circle of candles on her birthday cake. Gathered in the dilapidated recreation room, all the grey-haired men and women of the Live Oak Nursing Home clapped and sang Happy Birthday. "Thank you," Gigi muttered, waving with one hand, barely able to speak. Then she sat back down and accepted greetings from friends and health care workers. The room smelled of urine, but she was used to that.

Now 82, Gigi had suffered a mild stroke five years before; thus it was difficult to talk, smile or eat without assistance. Doctors thought she could improve, but the will was gone. Her only child, a son, had been killed in a plane crash twenty years ago. No grandchildren, no relatives. No teeth. No hope. No tomorrow. Life on the edge. A meager pension paid her keep at the low- grade facility.

"We have a new doctor coming in today," a worker told the group. Gigi paid no attention. She didn't need a doctor. "He's a volunteer working a mission on Saturdays. Have questions ready," said the social worker.

Later, the physician arrived to attend to the needs and complaints of the elderly. He seemed like a caring fellow, smiling, walking from room to room, asking questions, wearing a white smock and stethoscope. Gigi lay in her bed, television tuned to an old episode of *I Love Lucy*.

The door opened. Accompanied by a female nurse, the doctor entered. He was bald, just like her last husband who left her for another woman. "I'm fine," she grumbled.

"I'm Doctor McIntire. Are you sure there's nothing I can do for you?" he asked, as he lifted her chart.

"No. Leave me alone."

"Well, okay." As the doctor turned to leave, he stopped and looked at the chart one more time. Several minutes passed as the doctor seemed engrossed, turning page after page. Suddenly, for no apparent reason, he turned and approached the old lady's bed with a serious look and a glassy wetness in his eyes. He gazed toward her, then leaned over and lay his head near her cheek, caressed her face, held her shoulders and whispered softly, "Thank you."

"Huh?"

*

Cocoa Beach, Florida. Summer. 1974

Kids in school called him Garfunkel. Tall and lanky at seventeen, the boy had wooly-red hair that stood up defying gravity, scattered pimples and a straggly goatee. The only thing missing was Paul Simon. When he stood among his friends, he looked like a giraffe towering amid a flock of sheep.

But young Garfunkel had no singing voice. He was too shy and awkward for sports. Girls looked the other way when he walked down the hall, as though worried he'd talk to them. His friends, mostly dopers and rockers with boom boxes and pot in their pockets, usually took him along, much like a group would bring their puppy. It seemed they liked him, so he went everywhere and anywhere they went. Being liked was more important than being good, being successful, even, being loved.

He knew his mother loved him though she rarely showed it. She was always busy with real estate deals, working out at the gym, talking on the phone, shopping and entertaining her friends, women and men, plenty of men. Dad? Well, he had remarried and lived on the west coast in a city called Tacoma where his father had two step sons with his new wife. Once a year, for two weeks in the summer, he visited in Tacoma where he enviously watched the close relationship that had developed between his father and the other kids.

At home, life droned on. "Let's go, Garfunkel," his friends taunted. "Check that cool red Camaro over there in the parking lot. Let's go for a ride."

Willie, Mark and Garfunkel piled into the sports car while Brendon hot-wired the ignition. In seconds, they were on U.S. Highway One, riding north toward Titusville. They toked up a joint, turned up the radio, and sang rap music, jiving to the beat. Garfunkel didn't have to do anything, he just needed to fit in.

It wasn't long before the sound of a siren jolted the boys into reality. Brendon looked in the rear view and saw a police car, lights flashing. "Come-on," Willie prodded. "This car can outrun any cop car."

"I'm on probation," said Mark. "Damn, I'll have to do time. Let's run for it."

Brendon pressed the pedal to the metal and, in less than a minute, skidded into a palm tree head on.

Garfunkel was the only kid unhurt, so they took him directly to the police station where a uniformed cop read his Miranda Rights. He thought about a lawyer, but he didn't want to aggravate the police. They removed his handcuffs and placed him in a small room, the kind he'd often seen on TV reality shows. Sure enough, there was the glass window. He wondered who was watching from behind.

An overweight female wearing a brown suit and a pulled-back hairdo sauntered into the room, stared at the boy for more than three minutes before taking a seat across the table. She had a broad nose and big teeth, and wore a constant sneer. This was big trouble. His mother didn't need any aggravation.

Before uttering a word, the lady cop placed a small plastic bag of marijuana on the table. "They call you Garfunkel?"

"Yeah."

"Lookie here, Garfunkel. Possession, over five ounces," she said. "Stolen car." He knew this was bad.

"It wasn't mine," the boy pleaded. I just..."

"Went along. I know."

"Yes. Yes."

"You went along, and now you're facing jail time, juvenile court, fines and a pissed-off set of parents."

"Mom. My dad's in Tacoma."

"Talk to me, son. Who took the car? How many other cars? Whose dope is this? Who bought it, who sold it?"

The boy had heard about situations like this, where the cop offers a deal if you snitch on your friends. It's a good deal for the moment, but then you're labeled forever, and your friends abandon you like the plague. Some even get hurt. Really hurt.

"I... I can't tell you, Ma'am."

"Garfunkel, my name is Detective Morgan. I work juveniles. I've been doing this job for twenty-three years. I've seen you come and go inside this station a hundred times, over and over."

"Me?"

"Well, not you specifically. But hundreds just like you.

You're heading for the same life they've lived, struggling on the streets, job to job, in and out of jails, no one to love or love you, mistrusting everyone and anyone, dope, alcohol, and a long road of nothingness, until one day, you'll be too sick, too drunk, too mistrusted to even care any more. Then you'll either go to prison, and become some dude's cell wife, or you'll end up on a morgue tray wearing nothing but a toe tag." She leaned forward and peered deep into his eyes. "But there's something about you, son, that I think is salvageable. So let's go take a ride."

Garfunkel rode in the hefty woman's unmarked police car to the back side of a hospital. "Get out, son."

Moments later, he walked through swinging doors into a pungent-smelling room covered with white tiles; naked bodies — males and females — lay in steel trays wearing nothing but toe tags. He felt like throwing up, until Detective Morgan grabbed him by the arm. "Here, Garfunkel, watch the doctor here."

A man in a white smock covered in blood, with black horned-rim glasses, leaned over the body of a teenage boy with a bullet hole in his forehead. Garfunkel looked away, until Detective Morgan grabbed his head. "Drug deal went sour here. Watch, Boy."

The doctor then used a large scalpel to cut a vertical incision from neck to abdomen on the cadaver. Garfunkel's head went hazy, the room began to spin and moments later, he found himself waking up in the lobby couch. Detective Morgan came into the room with a cold wet towel and laid it on his head.

"This is your destiny, Garfunkel. A steel tray, a doctor's knife dissecting your drug-ridden body, and no one around to give a damn. I promise you, this is where you're going. All because you want to please your dopey friends who really don't give a hoot about you, no matter what you think."

It was a powerful moment for Garfunkel. "What do I do?" he asked the detective.

"First, you cooperate. To hell with the kids who won't help themselves. Don't let them bring you down. Second, if you have no schooling ambition, join the Army, Navy or Marine reserves. Go right into active duty out of high school. And never, ever touch a joint again, or any other drugs. And learn to say the magic word."

"What's that?"

"No."

*

"You don't remember me," said the doctor, as he looked into the old woman's eyes. She peered closely. Was this some fella she had a brief affair with years ago? *Naw. Too light skinned. Not handsome.*

"Sorry, do I know you?" she asked, bewildered.

The doctor spoke softly. "You saved my life."

"I did?"

"You were once a cop, yes? A detective?"

She nodded. Now, she knew he was on to something. But what?

"Your name was Morgan, before you married a Tennison, yes?"

This was getting spooky. She couldn't talk, so she waved her hand weakly. *Tell me more.*

"My name is Gilbert. But they called me Garfunkel in high school. 1974"

Gigi couldn't remember. "I'm sorry."

"I was heading for a lot of trouble, stealing, using drugs. You kicked my ass. You made me see the path I was heading, and because of you, I changed."

"Oh yeah?"

"When I saw those bodies, after you talked to me, I knew then I wanted to be a doctor. I wanted to help cure people. I joined the Navy, earned a commission and went to Med school. All because of you."

Gigi pondered, and looked closer into the doctor's eyes. She spoke almost clearly. "You had red hair? Kinda bushy?"

The doctor broke into a tears and grabbed her hand. "Yes."

"Garfunkel!"

"That's me."

*

That evening, Doctor Gilbert McIntire and his wife, Andrea, dined together at his plush home on Lansing Island, near Cocoa Beach. He told her about his encounter with Gigi Tennison. "She was the catalyst that altered my life from the depths of despair, to what we have today. Now, she's suffering, living like cattle, being fed, pacified and drugged daily to make life bearable for her, and for the staff."

"Gilbert. Something more is on your mind. What is it?"

"She has no one."

Andrea smiled and lifted her glass of wine. "Bring her home, Gilbert. We have the space, we can tend to her needs and hire on a part time nurse."

"I was going to ask — "

"You don't need to. What she did for you, you owe her at least that much."

"Thanks."

"I proud of you, Darling."

*

44

Giselle Morgan Tennison, aka Gigi, a retired police sergeant from the Brevard County Sheriff's Department, lived three more happy years without the prevailing urine odors of the Live Oak Nursing Home, the obligatory birthday cakes, the day-to-day boredom and the pall of unhappiness. For the first time in many years, she woke up every day with a zest for living rather than a wish to die. She returned to her painting, reading and making craft pillows for small children. With renewed medical help and therapy, she began to speak normally and managed to get around with the help of a walker. Smiles graced her face every day. She had been truly embraced in love and warmth in a beautiful home, made welcome by a physician whose life was so affected by hers.

One never knows what is destined to become a defining moment that paves the future road. Serendipity comes in strange forms. It did for a lady cop and a boy called Garfunkel.

The Beat of Henry's Heart

"Mediocrity knows nothing higher than itself,
but talent instantly recognizes genius."
— Sir Arthur Conan Doyle

Three old men and one women rambled through Beethoven's String Quartet Number Five like Geriatric Geezers trying to play the L.A. Lakers on the basketball court. Every ten measures they had to stop and start again, frustrating poor Selma who just couldn't keep up on the cello. Finally, Sid, the eldest, threw in the towel and complained to his friend playing first violin, "Christ almighty, Henry, can't we play something easier. This ain't no fun."

Henry smiled and replied, "Well. I thought it was worth a try. Okay. Let's pull out *Nachtmusik*. We all like Mozart."

Sid moaned and groaned. "Oy vey. We play that all the time. I'm tired of the same old."

Frustrated, Henry lay the violin on his lap. "All right, Sid, you pick then."

Selma sighed meekly. "Doesn't matter to me."

Fred, the slump-shouldered viola player, rarely said anything. He waited patiently, eyes to the ceiling.

Sid stood up. "I'm finished. I had enough. It's late."

At that, the four packed up their instruments, thanked Henry for his hospitality and walked out the door, agreeing to convene at the house again next Thursday evening. The last to leave, Fred stopped and turned to Henry, asking in his rickety voice, "Uh, Henry, I have this friend, of a friend. They know this twelve year-old girl, plays violin in middle school. They say she's pretty good. They want to know if I knew anyone who would listen to her play. How about it, Henry?"

"No way. I don't have any time for Twinkle Twinkle and little kids. You do it."

"I can barely hear any more. I promised I would ask. The mom ain't got no dough. The kid's father died. You know a lotta people, Henry."

"Forget it, I can't...geez, Fred, you know I'm not any good with kids." Henry saw he had disappointed his lifelong friend. Reluctantly, he lay his hand on his shoulder. "All right. Tomorrow night. Come over here, seven o'clock. Don't expect much."

"Thanks, Henry. And tell Dolores thanks for the coffee and pineapple cake. "

A successful man, Henry R. Hoffman had owned a dozen automotive repair shops throughout central Florida, but now had left most business matters to his son, Michael. Upon retiring in 2001, Henry dusted off his Ponormo violin and resumed his love of music after a lay-off of nearly fifty-five years. It was a struggle at first, but he still remembered the regimen of practice taught to him by Maestro Attillio Canonico back in the mid 1940s and '50s when he was touted as a prodigy worthy of Julliard.

Jonas Hoffman, his father, would have none of it. Henry came from a long line of highly skilled auto mechanics since the turn of the century, all of whom graduated the finest of schools and went on to become millionaires. Henry's mother, a pianist, knew her little Henry had a special gift from the time he played tunes on the piano by ear at the age of three.

His father agreed to giving him violin lessons, but his life's path was etched in stone: Henry was to carry on the Hoffman legacy and eventually run the business.

"But, Jonas, wouldn't you like to see Henry play in Carnegie Hall?" he remembered his mother asking.

"Bah," he answered. "My son's not going to be a starving musician. Hoffman Automotive is a sure thing."

And so, Henry's music took a back seat to the family business once he started college. When he married Dolores, he found a little time now and then to play duets with her at home. Otherwise, his violin remained in the case most of the time. As he acquired wealth along the way, Henry bought and sold violins as a hobby, finally attaining a genuine 7/8 size Panormo, made in Italy in 1782. Besides his wife and two grown kids, the Panormo — which he acquired in 1966 — was his most precious possession, worth far more to him than the fifty-eight thousand dollars he paid for it.

The next afternoon, Henry was feeling weak and suffering from one of his headaches. As he prepared to call Fred to cancel the child's visit, Dolores talked him out of it. "Come one, Henry. You'll feel better by tonight. You promised."

"Oh, all right. Give me one of those pills."

At seven o'clock sharp, little Emily showed up with her mother, violin case in hand, her dark hair pulled into a pony tail. Fred joined the group. Dolores, the doting hostess, served drinks and cheese. Henry was anxious to get it over with. While they chatted, Henry couldn't imagine the delicate child who looked no more than nine years old, holding a full sized violin. "Well," he said. "Let's uh...hear you play a little something there, Emily. Go ahead."

The child was obviously shy and nervous. He breathed deep, looked toward Dolores and lay his hand to his aching head. "Well, go on."

Her mother, Vivien, sat at the piano as the girl raised

the violin. Vivien started with a musical introduction which Henry found strangely familiar, so he stood to glance at her sheet music. *Vieuxtemp Concerto Number Four? You gotta be kidding me.*

Moments later, Emily drew her bow slowly as she started with the high D, sustained it four beats, then fingered the incremental scales until she reached the high E for eight chilling beats, showing a perfect vibrato into the high F. Hair rose like electricity on Henry's arms. He looked to Dolores, whose jaw fell agape. Seconds later, Emily hit the scales of four-note chords before the run of thirty-second notes into the highest registers capable of a violin, complete with perfect harmonics. Her tones were incredible. He swallowed hard, eyes welled, unable to speak. He could not believe his eyes and ears. This was the moment of a lifetime, a moment of witnessing greatness. His headache disappeared as he sat in awe of the small child with the huge sound.

Ten minutes later, when she finished the final chord, the room fell eerily silent. No one could speak. Emily seemed confused, as though people hadn't approved. Scanning the room, shyly, she asked, "Was it okay?"

Henry leapt to his feet as though he was in the center row of a huge theater, applauding wildly. Vivien smiled. Emily smiled broadly. Everyone felt elated.

Compelled to ask her questions, Henry went into an interrogation of sorts. "Come here. Sit. Child, who do you study under?"

"My eighth grade music teacher at school. He plays violin. My mom here, she helps me too."

"How much do you practice?" he asked.

"About four hours a day."

"What is your goal?"

"I want to play in Carnegie Hall someday."

"Who is your idol?"

"Jascha Heifetz."

"Heifetz? He's before your time. How do you know of him?"

Emily looked to her mother, who smiled in approval. "I've been coaching her in music since she's four years old," she said.

"Why don't you take lessons from a good private teacher?"

Her mother interrupted. "I'm a widow on assistance. We cannot afford lessons. But she has played in the youth orchestra. Mr. Stevenson is a good teacher, but he's very busy."

"What kind of violin is that? It sounds a bit tinny."

Her mother answered again. "Well, it's a school violin. They let her use it."

Henry gestured with his arms. "You should be playing in international competition."

Emily shrugged. Vivien shrugged. "Thank you," they both replied.

"Do you know any slower, simpler pieces, like for church. Maybe, *Meditation*, from Thais?"

"No. Not really. My teacher wants me to play concertos."

Overwhelmed, Henry pondered and looked over toward Dolores, who smiled and nodded. "Wait here," said Henry as he left the room. Sorting through his music study, he pulled a piece of paper from an old scrapbook, then brought his violin back to the living room. When Emily started to play a Bach Sonata, Henry listened a few minutes, then raised his hand, interrupting. "Child, come over here. See this?" He held up an old yellowed program from a Heifetz concert in 1947.

"Yes."

"Look on the back."

Emily turned it over and there was an original, blue-ink

autograph by Jascha Heifetz. "I met the great maestro after his concert in Miami. We talked. He told me to practice and practice, then signed my program."

"Wow." She leaned over and said, "Mommy look at this."

Henry smiled and proudly said, "Now it's yours."

She widened her eyes. "Really?"

"Yes. When I die, it'll just end up in someone's garbage. Now it will live on."

"Thank you, so much."

"And another thing."

"Yes?"

"You're going to take violin lessons from the best teachers in Florida, and in the world, if I have anything to say about it. Money is not an issue."

Hands to face, Emily's mother burst into tears. "Mommy, Mommy, it's okay."

"You'll play in Carnegie Hall, kid."

The room fell silent.

"And another thing."

"Yes?" Emily answered.

"You need a better violin. You can't compete against world class violinists playing a box like that."

"We can't..."

"I know. Here, take this one."

The others gasped. Stunned, the mother asked, "What?"

Dolores raised her voice. "Henry? Are you sure?"

"Consider it a loan. Look, I have another one. This is a genuine Ponormo. 1782. Rich tone. You'll like it. All I ask, is that you study and practice, and make your way to Carnegie Hall."

"Why are...?"

"I'm seventy-seven. I have arthritis and non-Hodgkin's

lymphoma always in and out of remission. Who knows? My playing days are numbered. And this violin must be played. It needs a good home for the next seventy years. Please, play it well."

It was a moment that changed Emily's life for all time.

*

Twenty-two Months Later

After nearly two years of home schooling, Emily directed most of her attention toward violin study, practicing five to seven hours a day, and taking lessons from the greatest of maestros in the world, including New York and Moscow. All expenses were paid, compliments of Henry Hoffman. Teachers had her concentrating on the hardest of violin music, including the *Brahms Concerto* and all the 24 Paganini Caprices. As time passed, Henry continued to urge Emily to learn a few simpler melodic pieces that pulled at the heart strings, but she was always too focused on the tough stuff.

"Don't forget, *Meditation*, from Thais," he said. "Or *Orpheus and Eurydice.*"

Now fourteen, she had become known as the local prodigy of Winter Park, Florida, a suburb of Orlando, where she played in a number of recitals. That summer, Emily embarked on a journey to Ibla, Sicily, the home of an annual competition of young musicians from around the world. With her mother as accompanist, she played the *Lalo Concerto in F Major* and won top honors. Henry had planned to attend, but illness kept him home to undergo chemotherapy once again for the ever-incessant rise of lymphoma.

As part of her winnings, Emily was awarded the opportunity to play solo in a joint recital of finalists at none other than Carnegie Hall. When Emily and her mother visited Henry and broke the news, the old man was elated.

Wrapped in blankets sitting in his easy chair, Henry motioned to Emily. "Come here, child."

Emily hesitated a moment until her mother nodded. Vivien and Dolores looked on as Henry, now more frail than ever, took Emily's hand and smiled. "How's my Ponormo? You like?"

"Oh, I love this violin," she replied, eyes wide.

"You know, little girl. I have two sons. Great boys they are. But they have as much musical talent as my bulldog. I always wished my kids or grandkids would go into music, but, ah well. But you? You are what makes my heart beat. I want you to know that. I love you, like I'm your granddaddy, I do. Now, I want you to go to Carnegie Hall, dazzle everyone, then work your way to Julliard, and dazzle them there as well. Will you do that for me?"

"I'll try."

"Maybe one day, I will hear you play in church, something not so strong, just beautiful."

"I will, I promise."

Three months passed. Henry's agonizing bouts of chemotherapy had reduced the cancer but weakened him terribly. Against the advice of his wife, he insisted on attending Emily's Carnegie Hall recital. With Dolores' help, and the help of a wheel chair, he would be able to travel. Indeed, he and his wife flew to New York City for the big day, to see his Ponormo on that stage in the embrace of the angel Emily, played to its fullest, enchanting the high brows of Carnegie Hall.

They arrived one hour early at the theater and met with Emily and her mother who were waiting nervously in the labyrinth of halls and practice rooms upstairs, behind the stage. She looked beautiful in her Cinderella dress with her dark hair pulled into a twist. Atop the table lay his Ponormo in an open case. "May I play it a moment?" he asked Emily.

She shrugged. "Well. It is your violin."

Henry held and admired it with a great smile, caressing the reddish-brown wood, feeling good about its grand journey and its future in the hands of this prodigy. For a few short moments, he placed the prized possession under his chin and drew a few variable notes to see if it was in tune and to savor its rich tone. Then he handed it back. "Good luck, Emily." He touched her gently on the cheek. "I'm very proud of you."

"I'm so nervous," she said.

"Not as much as the other recitalists. Remember that. You're the best."

He and Dolores hugged the child and thanked Vivien for being such a great mom, and for her devotion to music. As they headed for their seats in the Hall, Dolores pushed the wheelchair, touched her husband's shoulder and leaned forward. "Your mother would be proud, Henry," she said.

"Oh yeah. And why is that?"

"Well, you finally played the violin in Carnegie Hall."

"Ha. It's true, isn't it?"

Henry and Dolores sat in the audience where his heart billowed with pride and gladness at seeing his instrument on that famous stage, played perfectly by little Emily, the girl who made his heart beat. He leaned over to Dolores, held her hand, and smiled with a tear in his eye. When the final chord was struck, the audience rose to a standing ovation. Feeling somewhat faint, unable to stand, Henry tried to applaud but he could hardly raise his arms. Then the light dimmed, followed by darkness. The last sound he heard was Dolores' voice, "Henry, are you all right?"

The little girl who made his heart beat had been the catalyst for its final beat.

*

One after another, friends, relatives and fellow workers took their turns at the podium offering love and memories at the modest service held on the stage of a rented concert hall in Orlando, Florida, just the way Henry wanted. Sid, Selma and Fred now only a trio, played a segment of Mozart's *Lacrimosa*, from the *Requiem*, as Henry had requested. Finally, his beloved Dolores struggled with her emotions to say a few words about the genuineness of her husband, his love of mankind and of music, his utter awe of Emily and her musical talent. She drew a chuckle from the one hundred attendees when she told the story about him playing violin in Carnegie Hall, albeit six short and squeaky notes.

As she finished her short tribute, ready to invite everyone to her home for food and drink, she saw Emily stand from the center row. A long pause ensued as everyone watched. "Go honey," whispered her mother, seated next to her.

Dolores urged her to come forward. "You have something you want to say, Emily?"

Wearing a dark blue dress and small heeled shoes, her long hair draped over her shoulders, Emily came forward and stood at the podium, lowered the mike and panned the room. The silence was deafening. Finally, with a tear in her eye, she said, "I loved Henry Hoffman. I only wish I had told him that. He was like a grandfather to me. I'll never forget him. I would like to play one piece on the violin. This is for you, Henry."

Tears gushed like Victoria Falls throughout the audience as Emily lifted the Ponormo and, without accompaniment, played a slow, emotion-filled F Sharp with strong vibrato, then rolled peacefully into the most beautiful rendition of *Meditation* from Thais anyone had ever heard. No applause necessary. Clearly, everyone was touched deeply.

Dolores hugged the child, thanked her profusely and assured her she would always be welcome in her life.

Emily's mother thanked Dolores, then turned to her daughter abruptly. "Bring the violin here, come on, Emily."

With great sadness in her eyes, Emily handed the violin case to Dolores.

"What is this?" Dolores asked.

Vivien smiled. "Emily is so grateful to have had a chance to play on this wonderful instrument. If it weren't for Henry —"

Dolores interrupted. "That's Emily's violin. Now and forever. It's what Henry wanted."

Emily must have been certain that her playing time with the Ponormo was over, for she broke into tears. "Are you serious? I can keep it?"

"Never sell it, Emily. When you're an old lady, give it to another poor and talented child who will play it for another seventy years. It's worth far more than money. Will you promise me that?"

"Oh yes."

And so, the fairy tale ended and everyone lived happily ever after. Except Henry, of course. But he wouldn't have had it any other way.

Gigo's Crime

*"The biggest disease today is not leprosy or tuberculosis,
but rather, the feeling of being unwanted."*
— Mother Teresa

This is about a hardened criminal, a thief, killer, predator and sociopath without conscience, the kind of social parasite most of us fear and despise. We revel when he is sent off to prison so law-abiding folks can be safer and more secure in their homes. Americans wish to rid our communities of these people, lock them up, throw away the key, get them out of sight, thus out of mind. This guy personified "Bad." His name: Gigo

Arriving in the world was not of his choosing. Gigo never asked for the gift of life. It happened after a bet among drunken men. He was conceived in the back alley of a pool hall amid the ambience of alcohol, drugs and garbage rats. Nine months later, he was born in the waiting room of a local clinic, the fifth child of a twenty-three year-old woman who would eventually breed four more. His father's name was the same as that of his siblings: Anonymous.

Gigo's mother had been raised devoid of love in the squalor of an American ghetto, fending for herself since the age of eleven. Without skills, having children translated into public assistance like welfare, housing, food stamps, and medical aid. Making babies was more lucrative than any job she could possibly qualify for.

Gigo grew up in a two-story ghetto tenement where the aroma of garbage lined the sidewalks and the nightly concert of sirens and gunshots were as common as stray dogs barking in the alleys. The boy certainly received his basic needs of food, clothing and shelter, thus satisfying the perfunctory probes of burned-out social service inspectors. But he never experienced the most essential element in the emotional development of any child, usually of no concern to government inspectors: Expressions of love, approval and simple affection.

Gigo never felt a hug.

Gigo never heard the words, "I love you."

Gigo never confronted positive thinking.

Whales, elephants, lions, dogs and almost every mammal in the world experiences the love and protection of a mother from birth. It is as basic to the nurturing process as feeding off a nipple. It is basic to humans as well. Except, to some... like Gigo.

Other than breast feeding until the age of one, Gigo never experienced the tender and loving touch of a mother. Neither did he know a father. Rather, he was treated much like a pet in the house, provided food and shelter, and some medical care if absolutely necessary. Gigo never learned to use a knife or spoon. Rather, his mother would strew Cheerios or crackers on the table for him to grab, if he could. He had to share the ration of milk with his four siblings. If he was lucky, his mother would open a can of spaghetti from which he'd eat with his fingers. He didn't even know his own birthday. After all, birthdays required presents and cakes, unneeded expenses.

Without attentive parents, his role models evolved from the streets where older kids learned the rules of life by following the lead of even older kids. And so, the dilemma self-perpetuated much like it does in all urban jungles.

Men of all sizes, ages and colors paraded in and out of his life, all nameless, all drinking too much or smoking funny little cigarettes with his mother. None even so much as patted him on the head. Rap music blared from radios and sound systems night and day. By the time he started school, his skewed English routinely included ugly terms he didn't know the meaning of. Hardly a sentence failed to include the "F" word.

At eight, he began experiencing his mother's touch more often, ergo: the back of her hand striking swift, hard and mean. Her impatience and fits of temper were directed not just at him, but all his brothers and sister, so they were always afraid.

His heroes were Zeke and Moses, Big Diggs and Bamba, thieves and robbers, drug users all. They paid attention to Gigo and he, in turn, reveled in the acceptance he never received at home. Bamba and Big Diggs taught him how to break into windows and open doors from the inside. They praised him. When they ran from the police, he ran. When they shuffled and swaggered, he shuffled and swaggered. He liked the jargon and he basked in the sub-culture because he belonged, somewhere. They liked him. They approved. Thanks goodness, someone approved.

By age eleven, Gigo had become a mentor as well, admired by the eight-year-old street kids who had welfare moms and absent dads. He became an important dude, teaching the little kids how to steal, dance, talk, and break into cars and apartments.

Mama kept making babies so there was always food and clothes. But he liked gold chains, fancy cars and the feelings he had from marijuana and cruisin' in the hood. Nothin' was better than hangin' out. When Bamba went to prison for shooting a shop owner he gained instant fame and accolades. Zeke and Big Diggs said he was a hero. Gigo wanted to be a hero someday, too.

School teachers tried to tell him to follow healthy heroes like Kareem, Tiger, Colin and Dr. King, but they were as near to him as the planet Jupiter. He preferred the feel-good models like Big Diggs, Zeke and Moses.

Gigo watched Bamba and Big Diggs cut a boy named Madison behind a darkened convenient store, fascinated at the sight of blood gushing from his mouth and ears. He knew Madison from school, but felt nothing but awe watching him die.

When Gigo reached fourteen, another social system kicked in: Juvenile justice. Known he was, arrested a dozen times for stealing, breaking and entry, drug possession, vandalism, truancy. Like thousands before him, Gigo became just another face amid a relentless stampede of offenders. Because Mama dutifully appeared each time to assure the judge she would supervise, Gigo managed to remain on the streets. He rarely attended classes or studied, but he earned passing grades anyway as beleaguered teachers surrendered to anarchy. He entered eleventh grade without knowing how to read.

One night, he and a friend named Toodie were smoking a little cocaine, but they ran out and needed more. They had no money. So they waited by a freeway exit ramp near honky town where they saw a Buick LaSabre come to a stop off the ramp. Toodie used a spray bottle while Gigo started wiping the old man's windshield, without asking. When the elderly woman passenger reached into her purse to pay them a dollar, they smashed the window with a cinder block. She screamed. The old man tried valiantly to intervene, but Gigo managed to grab the purse anyway. He'd done it many times. Only this time the old man playing the hero role ended up stabbed and lying in his own pool of blood, just like Madison. Blood gushed. Fascinating.

By now, Gigo was a hard-core sociopath, feeling no remorse, no compassion. Mama had never taught him compassion. Neither did Bamba or Big Diggs.

A few months later, after Gigo was tried as an adult, he stood beside his spiffy public defender in a courtroom listening to a white-haired Caucasian judge sentence him to die by lethal injection. Finally, Gigo was a hero.

Another nine years passed as Gigo wallowed in a hot, bleak, nine by six, death row cell until all the tax-supported appeals were exhausted. In that time, no one came to visit him. No one cared, not even his mother. Then, he was killed — by the state.

Gigo's execution was not final justice for an urban warrior: rather it was the destiny of a hardened predator created by circumstance and conditioned by environment. We may feel that he had choices. But, did he?

During the political campaigns of 1964, LBJ initiated his great *War of Poverty*. It opened the floodgates of welfare and government support for millions of needy folks. We hoped to lift the poor and disadvantaged from lower to middle class status. Yet, the fatherless rate for births among blacks has increased, not decreased since that time.

Some say, the moment Uncle Sam offered hand-outs, a zillion hands shot forward and launched an entirely new perspective for many who would choose not to work for a living. In its wake came crime, social chaos, failed programs, budget deficits and a nation of Gigos.

Think about Gigo, his miserable, unsolicited, loveless life surrounded from birth by oppression and corruption, drugs, deceit and violence. That was his classroom. No options. His only source of self-esteem came within the gang. All his brothers plummeted into the justice system, just like him, products of a welfare mother who cared nothing about her babies as she sucked from a system designed to *aid* society. She was the daughter of a mother just like herself, fatherless, pregnant at age thirteen, drug-addicted at fourteen and destined to perpetuate the endless cascade of poverty and crime.

Like all of us at birth, Gigo was readied by nature for the love experience. Instead, he was filled with trash. His first crime was being born. His second crime was being assigned an irresponsible and unloving mother and no father. His third crime: Growing up in the hood.

As he amassed a predictable array of transgressions, we, the lucky babies, sat in judgement, spewing anger, wielding the banner of vengeance as though it were a solution to the problem. In fact, he was just another docket number on the conveyor belt of a failed system that perpetuates those very problems.

Who was it, really, that murdered that old man in the LeSabre?

The answer lies in his name.

GIGO.

Garbage In, Garbage Out.

Herman's Date

"Of all the worldly passions, lust is the most intense. All other worldly passions seem to follow in its train"
— Buddha

Dusk was turning to dark as the portly salesman pulled his new Buick into the driveway of The Buckaroo Steak House in Sylva, North Carolina. "Look, Herman," Nora said, pointing. "There's a parking space."

Herman had been ogling Nora for six months at the Super Walmart where they worked, fantasizing her formidable bosom, not caring that she was slightly overweight. After all, so was he. She was intelligent and well-mannered, nothing like that gold-digging hussy he was married to for twelve long years. This was his first date since his wife left him for a Hell's Angel biker the year before.

He had carefully selected the restaurant, not *too* pretentious, good food and most importantly; affordable. The dinner menu started at $7.95 for daily specials but offered an assortment of elaborate dishes as well, like steak and lobster at $25.95.

Herman escorted Nora into the foyer where they were greeted by a young hostess with spiked blue and red hair and very blackened eyes.

"No smoking, please," he asked.

"Sorry. All non-smoking tables are occupied. It'll be about twenty minutes."

"But the movie starts in an hour." He felt a nudge from Nora. "Oh well, anywhere then."

Herman and Nora were seated at a mid-floor table where couple nearby were smoking a cigarette. "This is going to kill my sinuses," Nora growled, as a waft of secondary drifted her way. (Cough cough)

"We'll go somewhere else," Herman said, steadying the table. *I hate tables that wobble.*

"No, we'll be late. Let's just eat here. I'm hungry."

While they perused the menu, a frazzled, redheaded waitress with too much lipstick jaunted up, pad in hand. Her name tag indicated: *Wanda*. "Hi ya'll. What can I get for you?"

Herman immediately spotted a silver stud in her tongue, and wondered why. "Give us a minute," he asked. Wanda pranced off.

"I want wine, Herman."

"You do? Well, of course. Wine. Yes."

"Don't you enjoy a good glass of wine?"

"Wine? Well, uh, sure. Sometimes, with a lot of ice. Sure. We'll order wine."

"Can we order a bottle?"

"Yes. Of course. A bottle." Herman opened the wine list and scanned the price column.

After several minutes, Nora tapped her watch and glared at Herman through lenses so thick they could be used to study amoebas. "Where is that waitress?" she asked. Herman trekked across the floor and found Wanda sucking a cigarette behind a server's station.

"Oh?" She feigned shock. "Ya'll ready to order now?"

No lady. We're camping in.

Herman's heart sank as Nora ordered a bottle of

Beaujolais, an appetizer of escargot and...what else? Steak and Lobster.

Herman ordered a $7.95 corned beef special and a glass of iced tea. Visions of Miriam flashed as he calculated the tab in his brain. *My God. This is gonna be eighty bucks.*

"I hear this movie is a thriller," she said. "Don't you just love Brad Pitt?"

"Yeah, well, I've never seen him," he replied. "Isn't he the fellow that played in The Terminator? Or was it Titanic?"

A pause followed. "You don't go to the movies much, do you Herman?"

"I like movies. Honest. Have you seen Casablanca? Or, uh, E.T.?" *My God, her bust must be enormous.*

"Uh huh."

He shrugged. "Well, I'm more into sports."

"What sports do you follow?"

"Well, I like football the breast. Uh, the best. Best. Yes."

"You know, Herman, it's nice sharing an evening with a man who's got something going on between his ears besides ideas of a roll in the sack."

"Really?"

"Most men refuse to see beyond my body without realizing there's an intelligent woman here. I sense you're different."

"You do?" *Geez, she caught me staring at them.*

As Wanda served the wine, Herman spotted *the curse* strolling through the door. *Oh no. Please. Sit somewhere else.* Screeching babies haunted Herman like a stalker; restaurants, airplanes, theaters, everywhere he went. They drove him crazy.

The waitress poured a few test drops of Beaujolais into Herman's stem glass while he gazed toward the foyer. Nora awaited his approval. "Herman", she said, gesturing with her eyes. "The wine? Please?"

"Oh, that's all for me, thanks."

Nora motioned to the waitress. "Go ahead and pour."

The sauntering foursome made the Beverly Hillbillies look like British royalty. An unkempt fellow in a Harley tee shirt toted a two-year-old under his arm while straggled-haired Mama tugged a soiled boy about a year older. Smokers both, Bubba and Emma planted themselves at a table beside Herman. Nora squirted a dose of Afrin in each nostril as Bubba and Emma kept their Marlboros burning during the meal. The kids whined. "Mommy, I wanna soda, I wanna candy."

The aroma of butter and garlic pervaded the air as Nora gobbled her snails, sipping wine between each swallow. Herman wondered if those marvelous mammaries were worth it all. Wanda served his corned beef platter and assured him Nora's dinner would be out in a moment. "Some mustard please, Ma'am?" Herman asked.

"Sho nuff."

"Ketchup with mine, please," Nora added.

Ketchup? With filet mignon and lobster?

They watched as Wanda rushed off to take an order at another table. "Why didn't she serve our food at the same time?" Herman asked, trying to steady the wobble. *I can't eat while someone watches me.*

"I don't know about you, Herman. You picked this place."

The shaky table tested Herman's patience, so he stooped on the floor to wedge a book of matches under one of the legs. That's when he spotted the cut-outs on Nora's open-toe shoes. *Oh my God, look at those bunions.* When Wanda arrived with the ketchup and mustard, she said to Nora, "Your order will be out soon."

Herman grunted from below. "Yeah. Well my corned beef is getting cold, lady."

"Sorry, sir."

Nora interrupted. "Herman, you're making my wine spill."

"I'm sorry."

Herman glanced over and saw the Clampett couple puffing cigarettes and grinning at him with yellowed teeth. They were eating chicken noodle soup, nice and hot.

"Shhhhluuuurp!"

"Herman, I think I'm going to be sick."

Herman choked on a waft of smoke, then saw that the waitress had brought a jar of Dijon.

"Shhhhluuuurp!"

He barked to his date. "I wanted plain yellow mustard. Not this stuff."

"Tell the waitress."

"This..." He sputtered through gritting teeth, "...is like asking for ketchup and getting Tabasco sauce. Where is she?"

"Eat, Herman, your corned beef is getting cold."

"Shhhhluuuurp!"

Bubba's baby heaved a plastic cup across the floor just as Herman cut into his meat.

"Waaaaaaaaaa!"

The shriek was like driving a pencil through his ear.

"Waaaaaaaaaa! Waaaaaaaaaa!"

"Shhhhluuuurp!"

"Don't you have any plain yellow mustard?" Herman asked when Wanda delivered Nora's steak and lobster.

"Sorry. That's all the mustard we have."

"How can this be? Yellow mustard is served everywhere. Is this what you serve kids when they order a hot dog?"

"We don't serve hot dogs."

"Lady, I wouldn't have ordered corned beef if I knew — "

"Waaaaaaaaaa! Waaaaaaaaaa!"

"Herman, I'm going to be sick." Nora said. "I can't stand this." (Cough cough) "My sinuses."

"Shhhhluuuurp!"

"Let's just eat and get out of here."

"Herman, it's a new ketchup bottle. I can't open it."

"Give it to me." Herman tried in vain to unscrew the cap. "Don't you hate new bottles?" he grunted.

"Herman, give it to me."

Yeah. Sure. She rapped the cap with a knife handle and opened it with ease. *Oh God, she thinks I'm a wimp.*

Nora shook the bottle furiously. "Herman, the ketchup's stuck. It won't pour."

"For cryin' out loud, Nora, stick a knife down there."

"Herman, why are you talking to me like that?"

"Sorry."

Using the knife, Nora jerked the bottle and emptied a huge glob of ketchup on her steak and lobster. "I don't like this place, Herman."

"We won't come here again."

"What makes you think we're going anywhere again?"

Oh well.

Bubba and Emma chomped into their rib-eyes and mashed potatoes, jaws chomping, baring mouthfuls of black-eyed peas and corn.

"Ugh!"

"What's the matter, Herman?"

"Look at that guy."

"My God. He's disgusting. Let's go, okay?" Nora's glasses now rested at the edge of her nose.

"Okay. First, I have to go to the men's room. Uh, ...cabbage." *Well, it was cheap.* "I'll pay the check when I get back." Nora tapped her watch.

It was a standard men's room with two urinals, two sinks

and two stalls, one larger than the other for handicapped. Herman considered the spacious stall but changed his mind. *Someone will see I'm not handicapped.* Once he entered the smaller stall, he wished he hadn't. The latch was broken and the door swayed out. The moment was compelling, no time to lose. He kept one hand on the door's edge to prevent his mission from becoming less private. Herman was a private kind of guy.

He heard a pair of men enter the room, one breathing heavily. Suddenly, panic! Herman's door slammed inward. "Yike!" "Occupied!" he shouted, pushing so hard that it swung the door in the other direction. It happened at the most inopportune moment.

"Ohhhhh."

"Sorry 'bout that, feller," barked a voice from the next stall."

Pants down to his ankles, Herman reached to pull the door back as a stunned teenager glanced over. Meanwhile, the heavy breather had seized the handicapped stall and unceremoniously released a raucous emission.

Ugh!

Problems were not over. The roll of toilet paper was jammed. No spin, no paper. Herman used both hands to turn the paper leaving the door to sway open. Paper peeled, shred by shred while he intermittently grabbed the door before it opened completely. Toilet paper...door...toilet paper...door...

"Oohs and aahs" emanated from the heavy breather in the neighboring stall. Herman nearly threw up his corned beef. More men entered the room. Herman continued peeling bits of paper, trying desperately to hold the door with one hand. *Dammit!* Suddenly, the door rammed his knees. "Yeow! No! Wait!" He leaped from the commode as a red-faced cowboy stood there, astonished.

"Sorry."

Yeah. Sorry my butt.

The heavy breather knocked from next door. "Hey theah, buddy boy. You got any extry toilet paper over theah?"

I want to go home. Herman ripped the roll from its dispenser and passed it under the stall. A minute later, he bolted from the bathroom. It had taken him six months to garner the nerve to ask Nora out, and now this.

"What took you so long, Herman," she asked, eyes bugged, hands running through her lopsided hair.

"Uh, crowded room. Sorry." He noticed the woman was alone with her kids at the next table. "What happened to the fat guy?" he asked Nora.

"Went to the bathroom."

"Oh." *Hmmm*

"Herman, the check." She tapped her watch. "The movie is in ten minutes."

Wanda was nowhere to be found. Sure enough, Herman caught her puffing a cigarette behind the server's station. "Can we have the check?" he asked.

"Oh? You're ready? Ya'll want a dessert or anything?"

"Please, Ma'am. We're going to be late for a movie."

"One moment, Sir. I have to add it up. Then you pay me."

Oh no. This will take forever.

"Waaaaaaaaaa! Waaaaaaaaaa!"

"Where's the check, Herman?"

"She said it's coming."

Just then, Bubba waddled up and stopped at Herman's table with a gaping smile. "Sure appreciate that, buddy boah."

Herman looked sheepishly at Nora then to Bubba. "Uh, don't mention it." *Go away.*

"Appreciate what?" Nora asked.

"Nora, don't ask."

Oh well. Who cares about boobs anyway.

Wanda finally arrived carrying plates to another table and dropped off the check. "I'll take that when you're ready." She rushed off.

"We're ready! We're ready!" Too late. She was gone.

Nora seethed as Herman pulled out a credit card. "Don't you have cash, Herman?"

"Well, yes, but I hadn't planned on wine, snails and surf and turf."

"What do you mean by that?"

"Nothing."

Herman saw Wanda racing from table to table as he waved his card vigorously, remembering her words. *"I'll take that when you're ready."* Sure.

Seconds passed like hours as the two stared at each other. Eyes shifting, Nora tapped her fingers nervously. "Where is that girl?" she asked.

Wanda detoured to another table to take an order. That's when Nora lost it. Her hair tilted awry as she leaped from her chair. *Well, I'll be. It's a wig!* Nora stormed across the room, attacked Wanda from behind, snatched the pad from her hands, threw it to the floor and screamed, "We want the check now, you...you..." Herman buried his head into his hands. "We're going to miss Brad Pitt! I don't like it when I miss Brad Pitt."

Hands shot skyward by an elderly couple in the nearby booth. "Please don't hurt me," pled the feeble man.

"Waaaaaaaaaa! Waaaaaaaaaa!"

"Hey, back off," Wanda shouted back, pushing at Nora's shoulder. Diners scattered like insects from an ant hill. Nora slapped Wanda across the face. Wanda slapped back. Nora's wig flew into the old man's bowl of clam chowder. *Splat!* The women grappled like two wrestlers.

Herman thought about running out the door, but it was

too late. He had to do something. But what? Not only was he aghast at Nora's black crew-cut hair, one of her giant falsies had flipped from her bra and rested under her neck as she lay on the floor. "Herman, what are you looking at? Get me up!"

I don't believe this.

A young restaurant manager hurried over asking about the problem. Herman blurted, "It's, uh, just that we wanted yellow mustard instead of Dijon. That's all."

"That's what all this fighting is about? Mustard?" asked the manager. "We have French's yellow in the kitchen."

Wanda shrugged indifferently, "No one ever told me. How was I to know?"

Nora seethed. "You...you. I oughta — "

The manager wedged between the two women. "Please, calm down," he said firmly.

"You atell 'em thar, buddy boah." Bubba's voice resonated from across the room. "You need any help, jes' call on me. I owe ya one, heah?"

No thanks.

"Here, Nora, you dropped this," Herman said, holding her sponge-like insert. Her bosom was now lopsided and half buxom, her face the color of a ripe tomato.

I don't believe it. Eighty bucks. Geez.

Looking like they'd survived a pacific typhoon, Herman and his bare-headed date staggered toward the door. A familiar voice bellowed from behind. "Hey ya'll. Something wrong with the service? You know, I work for a living, and you only left one dollar on an eighty dollar tab."

No yellow mustard, eh?

"Herman, we're late." Nora tugged at his arm.

The movie was sold out.

"Wanna come up to my place?" she asked.

Ah, what the hell.

Free at Last?

> *"Freedom is not worth having if it does not*
> *include the freedom to make mistakes"*
> — Mahatma Gandhi

Let's see. Peanut butter. So many. Peter Pan? Jif? Skippy's? I don't know. I don't know. Razor blades. Toilet paper. "Sir, do you work here?" he asked the young fellow wearing an apron and stacking shelves.

"Yes. May I help you?"

"Peanut butter. What kind should I get?"

The pimple-faced clerk blinked in disbelief. "Huh?"

"Razors. What's the best razor?"

"Uh, well, I use Gillette. I thought you were asking about peanut butter?"

"What do you do with this?"

"That's a frozen dinner. Stouffers. Lasagna."

"I cook this?"

"Yeah, you nuke it."

"Nuke? What's nuke?"

"Are you okay, Sir?"

In fact, Ernie was not okay. He had embarrassed himself, so he took one of everything and placed it in his cart and headed for the cashier.

"Coupons, Sir?" she asked.

"Yes? What?"

"I said, do you have coupons?"

"Coupons for what?"

She paused a moment and stared Ernie in the eyes like he was trying to be coy. "Forget it. No coupons. Too late." Ernie paid $27.66 cash with three ten dollar bills. As he headed out the door, the cashier hollered, "Sir, your change."

"Oh, sorry."

As Ernie held his bags on the curb, waiting for the bus, he felt an pressing urge to use the bathroom. The ride back to his brother's house would be at least twenty minutes; he'd never make it. *Geez. I gotta go. Where do I go?* He asked an elderly woman on the bus bench, "Ma'am, I'm sorry. I gotta, you know, gotta go to a toilet."

The bewildered woman became huffy and refused to answer. Feeling panic, still holding his bags, he walked into a Met Life insurance office nearby and approached the young black woman at the reception desk. "I gotta use a toilet. I'm sorry. Please, Ma'am."

She seemed startled. "I'm sorry, Sir, but..."

"Dammit, I'm gonna sh...sh...crap in my pants. Please!"

"But..."

A distinguished man wearing a parole-board type of suit walked into the hallway to check the commotion. When he saw the problem, he ordered the woman, "Give him the key, Nancy, it's okay."

Just forty-eight hours before, the feeling was indescribable walking out from behind the razor wire a free man after twenty-one long years of hard time. Ernest Lee Strunk swore he'd never go back. But now, it was total confusion. For most of his thirty-nine years, he'd been incarcerated in one place or another. No choices, ever. Not even where he went to the toilet.

Other than Victor, his younger brother, he had no

family and no friends. Sissie, his scrawny, ex-stripper, sister-in-law, had picked him up at the prison because Victor was in chemotherapy for lung cancer. Both lived on welfare and disability. Sissie was pregnant with her second kid, due in two months. She told Ernie he could stay a week or two until he found a job and could get a place of his own. With a five-year-old kid in one room and a new baby on the way, there was no space for another boarder.

Ernie asked her how to find a job. She told him to look on the Internet.

"Internet? What's that?"

"On the computer, there."

Frustrated and confused, Ernie didn't want to start learning anything new about electronics. He had promised to write his best friend in prison, so he started a short letter after everyone went to bed.

Hey Paulie,

How's it going? Hey, it's really great being out. First meal I ate a big-ass hamburger, cheese and everything, and fries, ketchup. It was like eating at the Waldorf Astoria. Feels funny making decisions and stuff. I ain't made decisions since I'm eighteen years old, except for deciding to do a stick-up. No more of that shit.

Still ain't got a job. No one wants to hire an ex-con. Vic and Sissie say I gotta get my own place. He's real sick. I don't know what I'm gonna do. My parole officer wants to see me working. Anyway, it's great being outa the joint. This time next year, you and I will hang out.

Well, I gotta go. Would you believe, it's almost midnight, and the lights are still on in my room?

Take it easy,
Ernie

The first three days and nights were long and nerve wracking. Sissie was always angry and screaming at her little boy and complaining about her husband dying and having no money. Ernie lay awake for hours in the night, thinking of the prison, the sights, sounds, smells, swearing to himself he'd never go back. Most of his so-called friends were either in prison or dead. No more drugs. Not even cigarettes. No more thoughts of robbing anyone. No thoughts of owning a gun, terrifying a store clerk, or mugging a pedestrian in the dark of night. No more. But, then, if he had no more thoughts of that stuff, why was he thinking about it at all?

Ernie lucked out. The next day, he walked through the gate of a landscape and nursery company and asked the manager named Zack for work. "I'm strong," he told the burly fellow, flexing his muscle. "I'm a good worker. I can do labor."

"Ever work with plants and trees?" asked Zack.

"No. But I'll learn. I really need a job."

"Okay, buddy. We just laid someone off, so it's eight bucks an hour. Fill out this form with your social and report to that guy over there on the golf cart. He'll show you around."

And so, Ernie had a job. He was happy. And, he was free. The measly two hundred and ten dollars he had walking out of the prison was half gone already. He figured out how much money he'd make at the end of the week and then find himself a low-rent apartment to bunk in for a while.

At week's end he visited his parole officer for the second time. Her name: Harriet Brown. She reminded Ernie of the actress Queen Latifa from the movies he saw in prison. Big woman, black, pretty. And weary from overwork.

"You staying away from drugs, Ernie? No booze either."

"No booze, no drugs. I ain't goin' back, you can bet on that, Mrs. Brown."

"It's about time you led the life of a free man, Ernie. You went in when you turned eighteen."

"That's right. And before that, in and out of juvenile detention for four years. Except for a couple months of freedom back in '88, I've been in jail all my adult life."

"That's because you shot someone, and shot at a cop. Lucky he didn't die. You get caught stealing again, you'll do the rest of the thirty years. Got a job yet?"

Ernie smiled proudly. "I got a job, Mrs. Brown. Down at Evergreen Landscape and Nursery, doing labor. Eight dollars an hour."

"Well, good for you, Ernie. I'll stop by and see you there sometime. I have to verify, you know."

He hesitated. "Well, I guess so."

Sure enough, the next day, as Ernie was planting palm trees, he saw Mrs. Brown in the distance park her car and walk toward the front entrance, pad in hand. Zack, the boss, met her at the gate and they talked for several minutes. Then, she ambled back to her car and drove off. He continued digging holes to plant the trees. When the day was over, he punched the clock and headed toward the bus stop. From behind, came Zack's voice, "Uh, Ernie, would you mind? I'd like to see you a minute."

Ernie stood at Zack's desk. "Yes, sir?"

"Ernie, you didn't tell me you're an ex-convict, for robbery and attempted murder, on parole."

Ernie's heart dropped to his feet. There was no response to make. No good response, anyway. "Yes sir."

"Ernie, uh, we work with the public here and there's a lot of money on the premises."

"Zack, you don't have to worry about me. I did my time. I ain't going back."

Zack paused with a saddened expression on his face.

Ernie knew it was all over. "Thanks for your help, Ernie. You can pick up your check on Friday."

When he arrived back at the trailer, depressed and angry, his brother lay sick in bed, head hairless from chemo. Sissie was in fits, cooking, cleaning, tending to the baby, and telling Ernie he had to get a place and go within the next day or two.

That night, he stayed up late and wrote another letter.

Hey Paulie,

The joint didn't prepare me for all this crap. Everyone's got a cell phone, I don't have a phone, only what Sissie has here in this dump. I got a great job, but got fired when the boss heard about my record. Parole officer told him. Now I gotta get a place, Sissie and Vic are on my ass. I don't know what to do. I went to employment, but they ain't got nothing for me.

It's ok. I'll get a job soon. It's great to be out. Kinda tough. Ain't easy.

By the way, how's Gordo doing with all the ink? Did he tattoo his ass yet? Ha.

Your buddy,
Ernie

Determined now, Ernie went out the next day with a pail of water, a bottle of dish soap and a bag of rags, going door to door in one of the nicest neighborhoods in Hollywood, Florida, offering to wash cars. He had shaved and donned clean clothes, some of which belonged to his brother, so he would look presentable, hard working and honest. Sure enough, he was hired on five times charging six dollars a wash and using garden hoses from each house. In one of the houses, he met Suzie Mclean, a girl he knew from high school around 1986.

"Why, I hardly recognize you, Ernie," she said. "Where have you been all these years?"

She was thin and attractive, wearing a halter top and shorts down to her pubic region and a tattoo of a butterfly under her navel. "Well, uh, been around. Working here and there."

"You married?" she asked.

"Naw. Never."

"I'm divorced. Married twice. My last husband gave me this house, he kept the money. You want to come in for some tea?"

Ernie felt his heart race. He'd never had a relationship with a woman. Should he? Could he? "Uh, well, I've got a couple jobs left. Maybe I'll come back after while?"

"Sure, honey. I'll be home all night tonight. Gotta babysit my neighbor's chihuahua."

"Yeah, well, okay."

Everyone was pleased with his work and he ended the day with thirty dollars, including tips. He figured he could make $150 a week, or more. This could work out. But his mind was on Suzie, betwixt and unsure, wondering if he should accept her offer. *Oh well, she invited me. Doesn't mean we have to do anything. She really is pretty.*

Later that afternoon, Ernie returned to the house where Suzie lived and rang the door bell. The car was in the driveway, so he figured she was still home. After a minute, he rang the bell again, then knocked at the door. Suddenly, her voice from inside sounded sharply. "Go away!"

"It's me, Ernie. Remember?"

"I said go away?"

Perplexed now, Ernie couldn't understand. Earlier, she was so friendly and welcoming, now this. "What's the matter?" he asked, loudly.

Her stinging voice left no doubts. "I looked you up on the Internet. I know what you did. Now, go away, please."

"But that was twenty-one years ago."

"I'm going to tell everyone in this neighborhood about you. And if anything happens, I'll tell the police..."

"Never mind, Suzie. Sorry to bother you."

With a hanging heart, Ernie walked the two miles back to the trailer, slammed the door then crashed on the sagging couch. It had been more than twenty-one years since he'd had a drink, and he knew it was taboo, but he was at the trailer, and there was plenty of beer in the fridge.

"Ahhh," he sighed after his first guzzle of Busch Light.

Sissie came roaring out of the bedroom. "What are you doing? Who said you could have any of Vic's beer?"

"I'm sorry, I didn't..."

"Tomorrow, Ernie, get a job and get out."

So, Ernie stayed up late and wrote another letter;

Hey Paulie,

Things ain't going too good. It's a bitch when you don't belong nowhere. Everyone stays clear of me like I had the plague. It ain't good. Now I gotta get out. I'll sleep outside I guess. I did pretty good washing cars. I just gotta make sure no one knows I'm a con.

Ain't as easy as you think out here.

Your buddy,
Ernie

The next morning, Ernie shaved and dressed clean before heading out with the bucket and bag of rags. He took the bus to Hollywood, near the same neighborhood where he met Suzie, then went door to door again, managing to wash four more cars. As he walked along toward the next house, a police car approached with two officers inside, then parked in front of him.

"What's the matter, Officer?" he asked.

"Are you Ernest Strunk?"

"Yes, Sir."

"Come with us, please. In the car."

"What did I do?" Ernie asked.

"Someone's house was broke into yesterday, over a couple blocks from here. Drugs, jewelry, money. You've got a record, Ernie."

"I didn't break into no house. I've been working. I'm on parole."

Ernie was taken to the police station and interrogated for three hours by a detective after being told his rights. Because there was no evidence to connect him to the burglary, other than his past record, he was released, but not before being warned that they were watching him closely.

"That's okay," Ernie answered. "I'm used to it."

Ernie was released at eight o'clock that evening. He still had thirty-four dollars on him from his earnings that day, so he did the forbidden and stopped at a bar and ordered three shots of whiskey and a Busch Light. Within an hour, Ernie was teetering on his feet, drunker than he'd ever been in his life, but not too drunk to know what he was doing.

Around the corner, attached to the bar, was a small package store. Ernie thought hard, thinking of all the struggles over the past week, making decisions, losing jobs, being accused of stealing, his brother and sister-in-law, the disrespect, no one to care whether he lived or died. No one, really, except Paulie.

Ernie walked into the liquor store, stuck his hand in his jacket pocket and thrust his fingers forward, feigning a pistol at the black man behind the counter. "I got a gun, give me all the money, now! I'll kill ya. You understand?"

Shaking terribly, the man complied, opened the register and handed Ernie a handful of cash. The man looked astonished when Ernie picked up a bottle of scotch with his bare fingers, then another bottle of rum and looked at the label. Extending his left forearm, Ernie exclaimed, "See this tattoo, Sir? I got this in prison. Did it myself."

The man nodded his head in acknowledgment.

"It says, Ernie. That's me."

The man shook his head again, puzzled.

"Don't call the police until I'm outa here. You understand?"

"Yeah, sure."

Later that night, as Ernie was writing another letter to his friend, Paulie, a knock came at the trailer door. Sissie answered. Ernie knew who it would be.

Within minutes, Ernie was in the back seat of the police car, handcuffed, headed for the criminal justice system one more time, jails, courts, lawyers, judges, and another sentence, just the way he wanted. He wouldn't have to write Paulie any more letters, for they would be together again.

And they lived *unhappily* ever after.

Victor's Dilemma

"Assumptions are the termites of relationships"
— Henry Winkler

Victor Jankowitz lived the good life. Perfect marriage. Good health. Two wonderful kids, now grown into healthy young adults. He owned a modest four-bedroom home in the suburbs of Jacksonville, Florida, complete with a twenty-foot aluminum boat and trailer and Johnson 110 horsepower motor.

Charles, his son, had graduated the U.S. Naval Academy at Annapolis and was serving his country on an aircraft carrier stationed in Guam. His beautiful daughter, Melody, was a bubbly sophomore at the community college studying to be a nurse and working part-time for a house cleaning service on weekends to make extra money. The light of his life, Melody was a good and loving daughter, though Victor didn't really approve of her tattoos. What the heck, it's what kids do nowadays.

He and his second wife, Maria, had been together for twenty-nine happy years, for better or for worse, in sickness and in health. She finally left her county job as a secretary to open her own art gallery. Maria painted with oil. Her art had been shown in some of the finest galleries in the country. Her shop kept her busy six days a week.

Indeed, the Jankowitz's were a God-fearing, Christian family attending church almost every Sunday where they enjoyed a close relationship with the full-bearded pastor, Orson Bullock.

A war veteran of Viet Nam, now retired from the Florida East Coast Railroad after thirty-five years, Victor spent most of his days fishing, playing cards with friends, watching sports and news programs on television and just hanging around. Sometimes he'd wander down to the Moose Lodge to drink and shoot pool with friends. Other times, when Maria was busy, he'd come home to take naps, or log on to his computer, read articles, send e-mails and look at pictures. Lots of pictures.

Victor didn't smoke, drank very little, gambled only nickels and dimes. He never cheated on Maria. He had no serious bad habits. Well, with one exception: Pictures. Moving pictures. X-rated *Videos*.

Victor could not resist the lure of porn, watching videos in the privacy of his secret inner world, men and women, or men and men, and women and women, in lustful, naked positions, copulating, sweating, screaming, panting. He surfed from one site to another in search of the most lascivious and erotic scenes, aroused beyond compare. Porn became his addiction, one that no one could dare know about.

Twice, he had to act quickly when Maria came home unexpectedly. He clicked off-line and pretended to be reading e-mails. Once, she asked him, "Are you all right, Victor? You're all red in the face."

"Probably my blood pressure, Honey. Would you check it for me?"

Lucky for Victor, it was over normal. "See I told you so. I'll take one of those pills."

And so it went. Other than Victor's little secret, life was near perfect for the Jankowitz family. Until, one day...

Maria was off to an art festival, sure to be gone past dinner hour. Melody had classes, then choir practice after school. Alone in his computer room, Victor sipped on a tall glass of lemonade as he began the hunt for more graphic eroticism, heart pounding, eyes glued to the moving flesh of those young and beautiful people. Blood pressure was at a boiling point when Victor ogled a young threesome gyrating in near-acrobatic positions on a king sized bed. As the camera zoomed close, he noticed a chain link bracelet on the wrist of the brunette. But it wasn't a bracelet at all, it was a tattoo. A familiar tattoo. He looked closer at the wrist, then the young girl's face as the camera pulled away, her hair flipping and swirling.

"Oh my God. Melody?" Feeling faint, breathing heavily, he looked closer. "It *is* Melody!" Quickly, Victor looked away, unable to watch. He he turned off the computer and sat in disbelief. "My Melody? Nooo. Oh my God." He ran to the bathroom to vomit, then sat upon the tile floor, weeping. He never felt more ashamed.

That moment, the tranquil world of Victor Jankowitz transformed from serenity to utter chaos. Now he faced a major disaster. Not only was Victor aghast that his sweet little daughter had engaged in sex acts on camera, he didn't dare tell anyone lest his shameful little secret be discovered. Yet, he couldn't do anything. He loved his Melody and could not bear to think she had turned to a sleazy life-style for the money. And here he thought she was working as a maid on weekends. How deceitful. What would Maria say? What would his friends say? What could he do?

He filled another tall glass with lemonade, this time adding a healthy pour of vodka and paced the floor in a panic, heart racing, sweating, pondering myriads of options. He glanced at the clock every five minutes. It was just a matter of hours and minutes before Maria came home. And then, Melody.

I'll say a friend told me about seeing you in the porn movie. No, then I'd have to identify the friend. No, I wouldn't either. I'll have to admit I saw the video. Maybe Maria would check my computer and see all the past downloads. She's good with computers. No. I'll just admit I watched the porn. Tell her it was the first time ever. Ah, no one would believe that. How do I handle Melody? Do I punish her? Do I rant and rave, cry and tell her how ashamed I am? How do I handle my own shame? Would Maria leave me? Would she ever trust me again? Would she think I was a pervert? Oh my God. Ohhhh my Gaaawwwd.

Victor poured another vodka-laced lemonade and took large gulps. He screamed at himself in the mirror, cursing, taking blame for not being a better parent. Having painted himself into the proverbial corner, he couldn't face his loved ones ever again. The twelve gauge shotgun leaned against the wall in the closet. Always loaded, he figured it would be short and fast. First, he'd leave a note, confess to Maria, plead for her forgiveness, then implore Melody to find the path to happiness without sin and debauchery. At least he wouldn't have to be confronted.

After placing the short, hand-written note on the night stand, he sat on the floor of the bedroom with his gun. He thought about the mess he'd leave, so he went into the shower stall, fully dressed, and turned on the water. He lay his shotgun against the tile wall while he guzzled the remainder of the glass of vodka and lemonade. Now blathering drunk, Victor sat upon the wet floor of the shower with the spray of water upon his head. Then he reached for the shotgun and angled it under his chin. But the barrel was too long and his hand couldn't reach the trigger. He thought about using his toe, but he'd have to take off his shoes.

He leaned his head back, shower raining, emotionally

exhausted, mad at himself for forgetting about the length of the shotgun. He couldn't get the images from his head, of his sweet Melody having sex with those two people. The room began to spin. As he began removing his shoe, he felt a moment of exhaustion, so he lay his head back again...and rested...and closed his eyes. Zzzzz

"Victor! Wake up. What in the hell is going on? Give me that gun!" Maria quickly turned off the shower and looked at Victor with the most puzzled expression imaginable.

"What? What time is it?"

"Victor, is there something you want to tell me? You know this is not normal."

He had screwed it up. He couldn't even commit suicide successfully.

"What's with this crazy note? Melody's doing porn?"

"I'm sorry, Maria. I'm sooo — "

"You're sorry? What the hell are you doing watching pornography?"

"Just let me die, please."

Moments later, Victor heard the front door open and close. Then, Melody's excited voice bellowed as she entered the house, "Mom? Dad? Guess what? Florida State sent me a letter, about a scholar..." The moment Melody entered the bathroom, Victor knew he'd been had. He imagined the picture in her daughter's eyes, seeing her water-drenched father on the floor of the shower and her mother kneeling beside him with a shotgun in her hand.

"Geez, what's going on? Dad, are you okay?"

He couldn't look at her. Maria answered, "Your father's fine. You and I have some talking to do, young lady."

"Huh? Mom, what's the matter?"

"Go in the kitchen. Wait for me."

"What did I do, Mom?"

"Just do it, Melody."

Moments passed as Victor dried off and Maria tended to his gun, making sure it was not handy. She asked again, "What happened, Victor?"

"I watch porn sometimes. I'm sorry. I know what you must think of me. But, I...I saw Melody, and I threw up. I'll never watch again, I promise. I promise."

"How do you know it was Melody?"

"Her hair. The tattoo of the chain on her wrist."

"Come, Victor. Time to confront our daughter."

"Must I?"

"Now is not the time to be a coward. Come on. Let's do it, now. We'll get through this."

"I feel so ashamed."

The last thing Victor wanted to do was confront Melody and wrangle a confession from her about having sex with multiple partners for money. Now it was necessary. He had no choice.

The three sat around the kitchen breakfast table. Utterly humiliated, Victor could not look Melody in the eyes without envisioning the images from the video. Melody asked, "Hey, come on, Mom, Dad. What's going on here?"

Maria took charge. "Melody, your father says you are in some pornographic movies. Is that true?"

Melody's jaw fell open. For several seconds, she just looked from one parent to the other like watching a tennis game. "You've got to be kidding."

"I want the truth, Melody," demanded her mother.

Melody looked to her father. Victor felt like crawling under the house. "Dad? You think I'm doing porn? Why, are you watching porn?"

Victor lifted his head slowly. "Yes. And, I saw you."

Melody chuckled nervously. "My dear father. There is no way you saw me. Maybe you saw someone that looked like me. But it was not me. I don't do that stuff, ever. How could you —? What made you think it's me?"

Victor pointed and spoke softly. "That tattoo, on your wrist. It's identical."

"Not me, Dad. Sorry. And, frankly, I don't appreciate — "

Maria interrupted. "Let's see the video. Come, Victor. Let's settle this now."

"I can't," he replied.

"Yes you can, Victor. You must."

With great embarrassment, Victor coached Maria through the web sites and found the same video. There she was, the beautiful brunette with the chain tattoo on her wrist, engaging in lurid acts with two men. Melody broke out laughing. "Dad. Look."

"What?"

She extended her arm. "Yeah, she looks like me. And she's got the tattoo all right, but it's on her right wrist. Mine is on the left. Look."

Realizing he had made a colossal mistake, Victor felt all the blood drain from his head. He lay his face into his hands, shaking, crying, "I'm sorry. I'm so sorry."

*

Orson Bullock had been the pastor at the nearby United Methodist church for more than twenty years, and had known the Jankowitz family since the kids were babies. He had counseled with them once before when their teenage son was caught having relations with an underage girl. This time, Victor called to talk to him about another serious domestic problem, but he had no idea what it entailed until Maria and Victor sat in front of his desk and spilled the story.

"Maria wanted me to come, Pastor. I wanted to...well, kinda keep it private. But — "

Maria butted in. "But, he loves me and he doesn't want to lose me."

Curious, the pastor asked, "What can I do for you?"

Victor spoke up, hesitating. "Well, Maria thinks I need a psychiatrist."

Taken aback, Pastor Bullock folded his arms on the desk. "Victor, I've known you a long time. You're one of the most stable and moral people I know. What's happened?"

Victor looked to Maria, then to the pastor. "I watched pornography, Pastor. Well, sometimes. Kinda got hooked since I retired, and all this time on my hands, with Maria here always busy and me retired. The computer was ...well, just there. So easy."

"I see."

"And, well, I thought I saw my daughter."

"Was it your daughter?"

"No, thank God."

Pastor Bullock pondered a moment and looked deep into Victor's eyes. "But that girl you saw. She is somebody's daughter, isn't she?"

The pastor watched as Victor and Maria looked at one another. Victor answered, "Yeah. She sure is."

"Just like your Melody."

"Just like my Melody."

A stark silence prevailed over the next few minutes. "Go on home, you two. I think this counseling session is over."

Victor never watched another porn movie. Time healed the wounds and all was forgiven.

And they lived happily ever after.

The Other Side of Bully

"Courage is fire, and bullying is smoke"
— Benjamin Disraeli

"Willard is a faggot, Willard is a faaaaggot! Ha ha ha ha."

Will Hoisington cringed at the chorus of the three boys and one girl, taunting, laughing, pointing, all led by big Stanley Bohrman, the school bully with buck teeth. Will felt the intense spotlight as other kids stopped in the hallway to watch and see how he reacted. He couldn't wait to bolt out the doorway and into the adjoining building to his science lab class. First, he rushed into the boy's bathroom, locked himself in a toilet stall and cried and beat on the metal door, his stomach in knots, bursting inside with anger, tears flowing from his reddened face. Then he realized the noise he was making and sat still, trying to remain quiet lest other kids hear him from outside.

As he emerged from the stall wiping tears, one of his science classmates entered and stood at the urinal. He nodded. The boy nodded, then said, "Don't worry about them, Will. They're just a bunch of assholes." Will knew the boy only as "Red." They were words of comfort, to know that not all the kids thought so lowly of him. "Why do they always pick on you anyway? Do you know?"

Just then the school bell rang, meaning they were late

for science class. Will shrugged to avoid the subject. As he started out the door, he reflected on Red's compassion and figured it would be all right to offer a short answer. "I dance," he said. "That's it. I'm just a freaking dancer."

"You should tell the teacher or the principal."

"Are you kidding? No way."

Eighth grader, Willard Ray Hoisington, had been studying classical music and dance at his mother's studio since the age of seven. Six years later, he was the only boy selected from Brevard County, Florida, to be in a student production of *Chorus Line* in Orlando's Bob Carr Theater. His mother was elated. Will was petrified.

After the final bell, Will checked the schoolyard to see if any of the kids were waiting. Venturing into the open without any teachers around was like being a wounded gazelle in the Serengeti with lions lurching in the trees. It was a short walk home, no transportation needed. But he had to cross the soccer field to get to the sidewalk. As the cars thinned out and most kids were gone, he started with a fast gait from the back building toward the yard. That's when he heard Stanley's dreaded voice. "Hey, faggot? Where ya going?" Then the others chiming in. Mindy Markham, Butch Margolis, and two boys he never saw before. "Faggot! Where ya going, faggot?"

Sure enough, there stood big Stanley and three other boys and one girl side by side, smiling, swaggering. They were predators. He was prey. There was no escape. He started running as fast as his legs would carry him. One of the fleeter boys tackled him from behind, following by a hoard of others joining in, hitting, smacking, kicking as he lay helpless on the ground in a fetal position covering his head. His books were strewn in all directions. One by one, they took turns with cannonball dives onto his back, laughing, howling, calling names. Will screamed and cried, begging them to stop, praying for a teacher or an adult to come by. It seemed to go on forever. Finally, Stanley called it off, "Okay, that's enough. He's had it. Let's go." They all ran back to the building.

Will struggled to stand, then hobbled toward the other side of the soccer field to the street, his face smeared with blood and dirt, ribs sore, his right arm limp and aching. It was a lonely moment, because no one cared, no one saw, and they all got away with it, having fun. All because Will Hoisington was a dance nerd.

No more!

When he arrived home, his mother was aghast. "Look at you," she said. "What happened?"

"The kids beat me up. They keep calling me a faggot and they all laughed. My books are still out there, on the ground."

"You're going to the doctor. I don't like the looks of your arm."

"I'll be okay."

"What kids? Who were they? Tell me their names."

That would be a death knell and Will knew it. "I don't know their names. Let it go. Please, Mom"

A divorcee and single mom, Myra Hoisington had a smaller child to care for, plus operating a dance school for kids. Life was a struggle for his mother and Will didn't want to be a burden. Then she said, "With that sprained shoulder, you might not be able to dance for a week or two."

Will shot back, "I'm quitting. No more dancing, Mom."

Astonished, she shook her head. "What? Will, you're heading for the New York City Ballet, or at least, Broadway. You're the best. Don't give it up now."

"No way, Mom. I'm through with dancing. Don't even ask." He ran to his room. "Leave me alone!"

The next morning, Will insisted on staying home sick. His mother sat on the edge of his bed, stroking his head with affection. "It's going to be okay, Will. You're strong. But we have to do something. We can't let them get away with it."

"I'll be okay, Mom."

"We have to talk to the principal."

Will sat erect. "Mother, if they ever got wind that I told on them, I'd be dead! No! I want to quit school. Leave me alone!"

Will stayed out of school for three days, praying that his mother would not go to the principal. He had asked her to transfer, but she didn't have the money for a private school. Will was stuck. He'd have to go back and face Stanley and the gang again.

This time, it would be different. He started working out with weights in his room every night. He learned the names of all the pro football and basketball players so he could talk sports. He practiced machismo in front of the mirror, swaggering and cursing and sparring like a boxer, talking trash to the chicks. Will was desperate. He had to fit in!

He applied for the wrestling team. The coach liked him because he was agile and fast. In his first match, he pinned another kid his size in less than a minute. He loved when kids cheered. They were sounds of approval and acceptance, sounds he needed desperately. Though his mother was devastated that he had dropped from the dance school, he felt he had no other choice.

Will accomplished what he set out to do. Girls liked him. He played sports, grew his hair funny, wore funky clothes and talked school lingo like the other boys. No one taunted him any more.

Four years later when Will was a gangly senior, his mother was watching the *So You Think You Can Dance* competition show on television. He walked into the living room and saw how engrossed she was with the talent and accomplishments of the young, rising stars, their exquisite bodies, perfect balance, flawless dance. She looked up to her son, "See, Will. That could have been you. Those kids will be rich someday."

"I know, Mom." He kissed her on the cheek, lovingly. "I love you too. I'm going to the gym, basketball practice."

"Be home before ten."

Will grew up to be a computer programmer for the Harris Corporation in Melbourne, Florida, earning nearly eighty thousand dollars a year. At the age of twenty-four, he married the former homecoming queen from his high school, the beautiful Megan Harbolt, a trophy, indeed. All the boys from high school had wanted her. Now she was his. They had two children, though the marriage fell apart for lack of love and common interest, just as his parent's had fallen apart a generation before.

Now thirty-five, divorced, paying child support and living alone in an apartment, Will was watching a reality show when the moderator featured a lonely woman from Peoria searching old friends from her high school yearbook. Just as she had hoped, seven of them were introduced on stage, one by one, now thirty years later. They hooted and laughed and hugged, catching up on old times from high school. Will thought about his own path in life, how it could have been different had it not been for a small group of kids that bullied him into changing who he was, forever. Then he pondered over the talent everyone thought he once had as a dancer. What a waste, indeed.

He picked up the phone. "Hey, Mom. I know I'm thirty-five now. But I'm in shape. Do you think it's too late?"

"Too late for what, Darling?"

He paused a moment, reflecting. "Well, you know, for dancing? This computer programming stuff, it's good money…"

"But you're not happy."

"Yeah. I watch dance shows all the time. I take my kids to stage productions. I wish it could have been different."

He envisioned the smile on her face. "Will, it's never too late. You do what makes you happy, not what you think others want of you."

"I know that now, Mom. But I gotta make a living. The kids — "

"So, make your living, but start dancing again in your spare time. Come to the studio, my assistant is marvelous. Come as often as you want. Bring the kids."

"You mean it?"

"Look, even if you don't make it as a professional dancer, you can always teach and choreograph, and be part of the culture. You will fit right in."

"Okay. Thanks, Mom. First, I have something I must take care of."

He had thought about doing this a thousand times. The time had come. The following week on his days off, Will used the Internet to search for big Stanley Bohrman. He wondered what he was doing now, if he was still the jerk he knew back in the eighth grade. Sure enough, he made a hit. Such a person was living in Wildwood, Florida. Then, he checked on Cedric "Butch" Margolis. He found him on-line through Facebook, living somewhere in Wisconsin. His picture didn't look familiar, probably because his head was shaven bald. He could not find Mindy Markham. He figured she had a married name now. He didn't know the other kids at all.

His next day off, Will embarked on a visit to Wildwood to find Stanley Bohrman, his childhood adversary, the bully who changed his life forever. He didn't know what he would do or say when he found him, but he was driven by an obsession.

Stanley worked as a convenience store clerk on a rural

road off Highway 44. Will parked the car, entered the run-down store and saw a corpulent, shaggy-haired fellow with earrings behind the counter. Tattoos covered both forearms. A customer had just received her change and was leaving the store. Sure enough, he had those buck teeth and jutting chin with the dimple in the middle. He was heavier now, but it had to be Stanley. A flutter of anxiety rushed through his body when he approached the counter. The fellow asked, "What you got there, Bub?"

Will's first reaction was to scream and leap over the counter and punch him out. *Don't you remember me, you dirty rotten...It's me! Will. The Faggot! You dirty...* "Uh, hi. I, uh, really don't have anything to buy."

"Then what do you want?"

"You don't recognize me, do you, Stanley?"

"Look if I owe you money, I'll get paid Friday."

"I don't want your money."

"Hey, man, do I know you? What's up? Huh?"

Two teens entered the store to buy gas. Will stood aside to let them pay, then resumed. "Does the name 'Will Hoisington' mean anything to you, Stanley?"

The fellow squinted, leaned forward and smiled baring his yellow teeth. He chuckled, "Yeah. I'll be damned. That's you. The school faggot, right here in my store. You're all grown up. I'll be..."

Incensed, Will felt the urge to jump the counter but refused to allow himself to stoop to his level. "Yeah. That's me, Stanley. Just like you, I have a name. My name is Will. I just wanted to see what twenty-three years did for you."

"Well, I got my problems, but you look like you're doing okay there, Mr. Fancy Dancer. What are you doing here?"

"I came to see you."

Stanley's face morphed from pugnacious, to inquisitive,

to dead serious. "Well, you saw me, now why don't you beat it? I got a job here."

"Things not going so well for you, eh, Stanley?"

"I said, beat it. Please, get out of the store. Okay?" Stanley paused. "Look, why don't you just go on." He obviously had taken an emotional turn.

This was the moment Will had hoped for. "I've waited twenty-three years. I think it's time you apologized."

Big Stanley paused, looked out the window, leaned over and placed his hands on the counter peering directly into Will's eyes. He wheezed like a heavy smoker. Will didn't move an inch. When a woman started to come into the door, Stanley shouted, "We're closed, Ma'am." She turned and quickly walked away. Stanley came from around the counter and locked the door. Now Will was trapped. His heart began to race, not knowing what was in this man's head.

Will thought Stanley might come after him, but he was wrong. Stanley sighed heavily then peered at Will one more time. "Look, Buddy. That was a long time ago."

"It wrecked my life, Stanley. I know we were just kids, but it changed everything for me. I know I can't take those years back, but I had to come and face you, as an adult. As a man."

The store clerk seemed to go into a seizure of sorts, taking deep breaths, and it worried Will. "Are you okay, Stanley?"

The big man leaned back against the counter and thrust his hands into his pockets, staring at the floor, obviously unnerved with a swarm of thoughts rushing through his brain. Will listened carefully as Stanley swallowed and spoke in a soft voice, shaking his head slowly, then crescendoing to frantic movement, left and right. With teeth gritted, Stanley said, "Look. You don't know what my life was like then. Don't judge me until you know me, okay? I know what I did to you. I have no excuses. But there are explanations."

Will zoomed in. Now he had his long time nemesis where he wanted him. "Tell me."

Stanley rambled on. "My family. My mother divorced my father and..."

"Hey, Stanley, welcome to the club. My mother and father..."

"You don't understand. Look. Uh, I don't know why I'm telling you this."

"Telling me what?"

"You see," Stanley struggled with his words. "you might think this is no big deal."

"Look, Stanley, lots of people had broken homes. So, what is it, man? Spit it out."

Stanley sucked one more long breath then looked Will in the eyes. "My mother came home one day and caught my father in bed, with another man. He was her brother."

The room went dead silent for nearly a full minute.

"What?" Will stood speechless. Stanley's face ballooned into a giant tomato, eyes glassy, spewing mucous from his nose and mouth. The two stared at one another, each hoping for understanding. Will was utterly bewildered. Neither man could speak. Both were sharing the pivotal moments that had altered their lives.

Now, it all presented a revised picture as Will's mind traveled in reverse, seeing the thirteen- year-old boy Stanley with the gang around him, taunting, laughing, pushing, hitting, in need of approval, yearning for self esteem at the cost of another's. He imagined life through Stanley's eyes, as it were a prism, the emotional trauma his mother suffered, and the feelings Stanley had for his mother and his father, and all that pride shattered into pieces, learning the ultimate secret of his father and the pain it caused him and his mother.

"I didn't know," Will said, in a whisper.

Blathering hysterically, Stanley leaned to the side and

placed his hand over his face. "My mother never got over it. I never saw my father again. Mom went into depression, and I was left hanging out to dry. No one knew. I never told anyone." Will watched as Stanley used a paper towel to wipe his eyes. "Look at me, Will. I'm a damned junkie living hand to mouth and you're a big success. What are you complaining about?"

Will muttered, "I don't know what to say."

"Look, man. You want an apology? I'm sorry, okay? I'm really sorry. I was wrong. I can't take it back." Stanley wept aloud and moved closer to Will.

"It's okay, Stanley." Will wrapped his arms around Stanley as he continued to bawl. Will couldn't contain his own emotions and began sobbing with him. He had never considered what negative forces Stanley may have lived through. He thought he would be vindicated if he could only garner an apology, but somehow, the vindication was lost in a deep hole somewhere and he did not feel good about it at all. He knew what he had to do.

"It's me who owes an apology. I'm sorry, Stanley. We're okay now, man. I didn't know. I'm really sorry."

A week later, Will was reading a story from a Charles Dicken's book to his seven-year-old son who he was keeping overnight. When the child pointed to picture of Scrooge, he said, "He's a mean old man, isn't he, Daddy?"

Will responded, "Maybe not, Billy. You haven't lived in his shoes, so be careful about what you say about others until you know their life's story."

Little Billy laughed. "Okay. Bah humbug."

Will hugged his child. "Right, son. Bah humbug to you too."

Mother's Day at the Book Store

"Family is the most important thing in the world"
— Diana, Princess of Wales

The pace was more hectic than she ever imagined. Another book signing, the fourth in five days; Borders, Barnes & Noble, Books-A-Million. Radio and television interviews, speeches, writers conferences, libraries and conventions. The notoriety was wonderful and so were the royalty checks, but oh, if only she could only retreat for a few days of seclusion and relaxation. Then, back to the keyboard.

Beverly Armand-McNutt stood before her bathroom mirror, leaned forward and checked out every wrinkle in her brow, the crow's feet, the sagging jowls and decided once and for all she would break down and pay for a comprehensive nip and tuck. After all, she had earned it. Her newly published, Christian-based romance novel was finally on retail book shelves along side of famous writers like Anne Rice, John Grisham and Debbie Macomber.

It had been a long journey, from jailbird to Walmart greeter to real estate agent to renowned author, but she stuck it out, knowing that her writer's flair would pay off one day.

All it took was a little talent and a lot of perseverance. But fame and fortune didn't come easy.

For thirty-five long years, Beverly struggled with alcoholism and depression, losing three husbands to divorce before the age of forty-five, plus custody of her two sons with husband number two. To this day, they would have nothing to do with her. Her life had hit bottom at age fifty-four when she ended up in the psychiatric ward of the Orange County Jail, in isolation wearing suicide-proof garb and no underwear, charged for the second time with DUI and hit and run. She lost everything, money, property, job, respect and self-esteem.

She had all the chances. A good and loving family, homecoming queen of Virginia Beach High School in 1965, basketball star, scholarship to Clemson University and a degree in marketing, and a job with one of the premier representative firms in the state of Virginia. Much like thousands of others, her life crashed over a man's rejection when she was only twenty-five. All her friends had told her that an affair with the boss could only lead to disaster, especially when he was married. It was like trying to recover the sense of love she once felt, that addiction to feeling wanted, to feel whole again.

Jail was the most horrible experience of her life. Nearly one full year inside steel cages with women howling and screaming, fighting and crying. Crappy food, no privacy, no medical relief for migraines, musty and putrid odors, the incessant sounds of rattling keys, and being ordered around like a dog. She had reached hell on earth. It couldn't be worse. But the time gave her eleven months and one week of sobriety with which to think and consider how to get her life in order. It also revived her faith in God and brought her closer to Jesus Christ, thanks to a black woman minister who had befriended her from the beginning of her jail sentence. With

God and Jesus by her side, she felt loved. When those gates opened, she wasn't going to slide backwards.

That was eight years ago. From the day she left jail, Beverly kept a copy of the King James Bible with her at all times. She prayed daily, attended church and lived a clean and moral life. Attempts to contact her two boys — now young men — were met with hang-ups and no responses to her letters. So, she moved on. They had been raised with a loving step-mother, so they didn't need her, a washed out recovering drunk with a criminal record.

Another state, another life. Florida was warm in winter and no one knew her there, so she moved to the Space Coast where she could watch the mighty rockets lift off into space. While working at Walmart, and receiving disability for her bi-polar diagnosis, she attended real estate school and went to work as a sales agent the day she received her license. Though she lived alone with two cats in a modest apartment in Titusville, Florida — just across the river from the Kennedy Space Center — she made good friends and enjoyed a better life than she had known since she started drinking at the age of twenty-seven.

During long periods of solitude, Beverly found solace in her writing. Fiction had always fascinated her. She loved making up the stories, the characters, the struggles. After all, it was like converting true life into make believe.

She was thrilled when her first short story was published in a prominent Christian magazine. After receiving a check for $500, she could be considered a professional writer. Her critics and friends urged her to write a book. The ideas and the writing came easy to her.

She never thought it would happen. Other writers told her the chances of getting an agent and then getting published by a major publisher was one in a thousand. So when that phone call came with a contract offer for an advance of $10,000 and an agreement to write two books a year, Beverly rode the clouds. Friends at the office threw her a party. When her first book signing was scheduled, she thought she had reached heaven. She could hardly believe that ordinary people loved her writing and that, despite her life's troubles, she would become an overnight millionaire at the age of sixty-three.

She pinned her bleached-blonde hair to the top of her head like an eagle's nest then headed to the Melbourne Barnes & Nobles. It was her signature style, wearing a peasant skirt, sandals and wispy strands of hair falling over the sides of her face. The public had never seen her with long hair down her back. She greeted the store manager and took her place at the signing table, where stacks of books awaited her pen. A line of fans had already formed out the door before the store was opened. She glanced at the sandwich sign on the floor that featured her photograph peering into the eyes of patrons and thought, if only her mother and father could see her now.

The first woman customer came to the table, then a second, third, tenth, twentieth, thirtieth — more than two hundred books signed at one sitting. Finally, after two hours, the line was nearing its end and Beverly was tired.

"May I offer another iced mocha?" asked the store manager.

"No thank you. I'll be leaving soon."

The last woman approached the table, book in hand. Holding her pen, Beverly barely looked up. "Hi. Your name please?"

"Brigitte. Just sign it to Brigitte, please," replied the soft female voice.

The name triggered an instant pause. Beverly pondered it a moment, then started to sign. Halfway through, she looked up into the eyes of the young lady, very tall, about thirty, soft features, sad eyes. She said, "I knew a Brigitte, once. Not a common name these days."

Beverly finished the signing, smiled and handed the book over, at which time the woman stood there, her eyes turning into pools, lips quivering. Confused, Beverly asked. "What's the matter, Miss? Are you all right?"

The woman barely could choke her response. "Uh, well, I'm your daughter."

*

That moment, Brigitte felt like her heart had stopped. She looked into the esteemed author's eyes and saw the mirror image of herself in another thirty-three years. She could barely stop herself from sobbing like a sniveling idiot. More importantly, she braced herself for a reaction. Would she be startled? Would she deny? Would she stand and run off, telling her to be gone and leave her alone, forever? Would she be angry that she was discovered, exposed? Would she worry that this was a shakedown, that she would want something from her? Apologies? Money? Love? Retribution?

Speechless, Beverly Armand-McNutt sat rigid with the corners of her mouth downward, staring into Brigitte's eyes in a state of wonder. Her hand began to quiver, like Parkinson's disease. For several long minutes, nothing was said between the two women, until Brigitte finally stepped forward and touched her hand. In an attempt to comfort, she said, "I only want to know you. That's all. It's okay. I understand." She could see that her words were reassuring. Beverly relaxed and sat back in her chair, still in eye contact, still in awe.

Finally, the older woman choked on her words. "I never thought I'd see this day."

Brigitte saw anguish in her eyes and tried to allay any fears. "I, I...don't want — "

"You're so beautiful. So, beautiful."

Brigitte smiled. "I'm thirty. I'm a stock broker, in New York."

"Do you have children?"

Brigitte smiled widely. "Yes, you have a grandson. He's five. Name is Charles."

Beverly sucked a deep breath. "Wow."

The ice had been broken. Now it was time to move on. "Can we talk? Would you mind?"

"Oh, yes. Of course. I have to get out of the store. Too many fans here. Meet me at Starbucks. Down the street here, on New Haven."

Thirty minutes later, as she sat at an outside table sipping on a Chai Tea Latte, Brigitte checked her watch wondering if her newfound mother would be standing her up. Finally, a white Lexus parked three spaces away and the aging lady emerged, her wild hair in place, make-up applied, brightened and cheery.

"How did you find me?" Beverly asked.

"I hired a private investigator. They found the original birth certificate, from Richmond."

"I see."

"I was only three months old when you gave me up for adoption. I want you to know, I have had wonderful adoptive parents. But, there are so many questions."

"I can imagine. I'll try to answer."

"Like, who was my biological father?"

Beverly stiffened, then looked left and right. Brigitte could see that the question was a setback. Did she anger her mother? Embarrass? Offend? She didn't want to screw this up.

Beverly began with an explanation, saying she owed it to her daughter. "I had a lot of problems back in those days," she said, apologetically. Brigitte listened, intensely. "My first marriage, well, was a mistake. Only lasted a year, then I was single for ten years."

"But, during that time I was conceived, yes?"

Beverly ignored the question and rambled on, holding her coffee cup with both hands. "They said I was bi-polar, or something. I got sick a lot. Honestly, I...uh, had a problem holding down a job, and drinking."

"I read about you on line. There's have been a couple of biographies— "

"I know. Yes, I drank. I'm sober now for almost nine years."

"So, who's my father?"

Beverly looked her directly in the eyes and responded in a quiet, stiff voice. "I don't know."

The answer stunned Brigitte. She thought her mother might be evasive and would try to keep the secret intact. But she hadn't counted on this. "Why? How can you not know?"

"Well, Brigitte. You want honesty, here's honesty. I slept around in those days. I can go into all the excuses and psychological baloney, but the truth is, your father could be any one of three of four guys. I can see, for sure, you're not the daughter of Bernie Hollis."

"How do you know?"

"Because he was black."

Brigitte was more determined than ever now. "Do you know the names of the others?"

"One. His name was Reginald Fordham. Reggie, actually. Savannah, Georgia. Much older than me. Trucker. Heavy smoker. He's probably dead by now."

"Why?"

"Don't know. Just got a hunch."

"The others?"

"One guy's name was Truman. First name, Truman.

Everyone called him "True." The other guy, I never did catch his name. He was a one-night stand after meeting in a bar. Sorry, that's all I know. I'm being as honest as I can."

Brigitte wanted to make the best of it. "That's okay, uh, Beverly. Mrs. McNutt. I hope you don't mind — "

"Beverly. For now. Just call me Beverly. Maybe, after we get to know each other a little more."

"I understand, Beverly."

"You were three months old. I tried to take care of you, but you were always with the neighbors or a baby sitter of some kind while I tried to work. I wasn't a good mother. I couldn't give you a good life."

"I understand. It's okay. You did the best you could."

"I went to jail, a couple times. I finally straightened out my life. I'm okay now."

"I know. What happened? How did you do that?"

"Jesus. I accepted Jesus in my heart. I love God, and pray every day. I live a Christian life now. And look at me. You would not have been proud of me before, but I'm a successful woman now."

"That's great. Thank you for sharing. Thank you for talking to me."

"Can I ask you a question?"

"Sure." Brigitte was curious. What would her mother ask of her?

"You have a picture of my grandson, Charles?"

Brigitte's heart billowed that she cared enough to ask. When she showed the photograph of her small boy, Beverly asked another question. "His daddy? What does he do?"

Brigitte braced herself. This was the moment of truth. "To be honest, I don't know?"

Beverly furrowed her eyebrows, "How can you not know what your husband does?"

"I never met his father."

"Huh?"

"My partner's name is Norma. She's a lawyer. I had the baby through artificial insemination." Brigitte watched the woman's face drop. She had to complete the revelation. "I'm gay."

*

The shock was almost as powerful as the moment when Brigitte stood at the book signing table; "Hello, I'm your daughter." *My God! My daughter is gay?* All Beverly could think about was her Christian teachings, that homosexuality was a choice, unnatural, sinful, wrong. But, here was this beautiful woman, her daughter, sharing her heart and her feelings, craving acceptance, openly admitting she was a homosexual, yet a proud mother. She pondered her own journey of more than sixty years and how often she craved for acceptance throughout her life. Beverly saw the anxiety in Brigitte's face and wished she could reach over and comfort her, but the force of righteousness held her back.

"I, uh, don't know what to say."

"It's okay, Beverly. I'm used to it. If you want, I'll leave."

Wracked with conflict over love, hate, right and wrong, and the string of errors she had made throughout her life, Beverly did not want to make another mistake. "No, no. Stay. Please."

"If I offended you because of your religion — "

Beverly dismissed the question without an answer. Instead, she said, "You should know. You have two brothers."

Brigitte stopped as she raised the cup to her lips. "I do?"

"Don't worry, honey, they're not bastards. Stephen, my second husband, took custody of them when we divorced. He was right to do that. I was a drunk. They were just four and seven then. Today, they're in their mid twenties."

"How, where...?"

"They live in Fresno, California, the last I heard. They won't have anything to do with me."

"Names?"

"Freddie. He's the oldest. Jamie, he's three years younger. Last name is Vasquez."

"Mexican?"

"Cuban."

Beverly sipped her coffee while she watched Brigitte ponder and look around at the strip shopping plaza. Silence had set in, as though there was nothing more to say. Finally, Brigitte asked, "So, what now? I guess I accomplished my mission. I don't know what to do."

Beverly felt a sudden shroud of warmth, compelled to bestow all the love on her child that she could possibly make up for. She took Mryna's hand and smiled, "I want to meet my grandson. I really don't want this to end. I don't care that you're gay. At first, I — "

"I understand. It was a shock. It's okay."

"Well, it's a full day of surprises. But I don't care. I really don't. I don't want this to end."

One would think Brigitte had just won a million dollars as she exploded into tears. Beverly exploded with her. Folks in a nearby table looked on as the two women stood up and hugged, and wept and apologized. "I'm sorry, Brigitte. I'm so sorry."

"There's nothing to apologize for, Beverly."

As they composed themselves and sat back on the wrought iron chairs, Beverly giggled, "Look at me. My mascara is running. So is yours." They smiled, happily. Then Beverly asked, "Where is little Charles? Is he here in town with you? I'd love to see my grandson."

At that, Brigitte turned around, faced the parking lot and waved. From a parked, black SUV, a blonde woman wearing jeans and a red top emerged from the passenger side. As she walked around the car, Beverly could see that she was holding the hand of a small, bushy-headed boy in shorts, tee shirt and sneakers. They started walking toward Starbucks. Beverly's eyes welled into pools of joy as she was about to meet a grandson she never thought — in a million years — would become a part of her life.

And they all lived happily ever after.

Ripples of 9/11

"As long as there are sovereign nations
possessing great power, war is inevitable"
— Albert Einstein

Remember the name: Marianne Lynn Ormond.

New York City Firefighter, Sean Michael McMillan, 24, had graduated the academy only two months before. Now, he was battling the scene of a lifetime. The second tower of the World Trade Center had just swallowed a Boeing 757 somewhere around the eightieth floor. Chaos prevailed. Sirens blared everywhere. Dust and debris rained upon cops and firefighters as Sean leaned over to get a better grip on the hose. He knew many people were dying inside the two buildings where fires raged. A soot-covered supervisor shouted orders at him, but he was distracted by the sudden and approaching screams from above. He looked up. *Whoosh.* A split second image of flailing arms and legs flashed, then... *Kawhack! Kaplop!* The body slammed into the pavement and bounced as if on a trampoline. Blood splattered on Sean's face mask. When the woman landed a second time, she lay in twisted, mangled heap, face up in a blank stare.

Stunned, the young fireman fixated on the dead woman, ignoring his irate supervisor. "Sean, what's the matter with you?" He couldn't stop gazing at the corpse, twisted, head reversed, blood pooling from her body yet her face was intact. Those horrid seconds went into instant replay, *Whoosh... Kawhack.... Kaplop.* He stared, stomach knotted, his body in convulsions. He lost control — "*Eiiigggghhh!*"

He felt a man's arms around him like a bear hug, but he couldn't stop screaming. "Calm down, Sean," shouted the boss. "Easy, boy." As though an evil outside force had invaded his body, Sean could not control the frenetic outburst.

"*Eiiigggghhh! Eiiigggghhh!*" Sean wished he could run away, anywhere. "*Eiiigggghhh!*" He looked to the sky and saw a man falling, legs flailing, descending at 100 miles per hour just one hundred feet away. *Kawhack ... Kaplop*

"*Eiiigggghhh!*" Powerful arms wrapped tightly around his body as the elder fireman pulled him away, shouting, "Get over here, Jose. Sean's lost it."

"*Eiiigggghhh!*"

*

With the tray table down, Seymour Morris Abramson labored over a crossword puzzle aboard a British Airways flight from London to Philadelphia. Ailish, his Irish-born wife, was sound asleep, head resting on a pillow. That's when the pilot announced on the intercom that their flight was being diverted to Canada. No other information.

What?

An hour later, the plane landed in the small town of Moncton, New Brunswick. Passengers were confused over the diversion until the pilot finally announced that two airplanes had mysteriously crashed into the World Trade Center in New York. All airports were being closed in the United States.

"Damn! Wouldn't you know it," Seymour exclaimed,

checking his watch. "You've got a doctor's appointment tomorrow. Margaret is coming to meet us at the airport. I hope she knows."

"It'll be all right, Seymour," said Ailish, calming her husband. "Don't get excited. Please. Your blood pressure."

"Damn, where in the hell are we? Moncton? Where's that? What a way to end a vacation."

Two hours later, the elderly couple was herded with hundreds of other passengers from twenty-two displaced airplanes into a giant hockey coliseum in the center of this strange town. Red Cross workers scurried about, setting up tables. Ailish glanced upward and gasped. "Seymour, look at that big TV screen."

"Oh my God!" he exclaimed as he watched the repeated videos of airplanes crashing into the twin towers. "There must be thousands of people there." Insert photos of Osama Bin Laden appeared on the screen as news reports cited him and al Qaeda, as the source of the worst attack on the United States since Pearl Harbor.

"This is terrible," said Ailish. They watched hoards of helpless, confused passengers trying to find their way into the seating tiers.

For three long days, more than three thousand passengers ate Red Cross-provided sandwiches and used rows of army cots for sleeping on the floor of the arena. Everyone anxiously awaited news from their respective airlines when the airports would be reopened.

"I don't feel good," said Seymour, from his cot.

"I'll get a doctor."

"No. No, I'm just upset."

"I told you we should have bought a cell phone. We have no way to call Margaret."

"Please, Ailish. Not now."

The announcement finally came that all airports were

being reopened and air travel would resume. When Seymour asked the British Airways representative when they could re-board, he said the plane was not going on to Philadelphia. Rather, it was returning to the U.K.

"You're abandoning us here?" Seymour asked in a loud voice.

"Sorry, Sir."

"How do we get home?"

"Well, you can board if you want to go back to England."

"We have to go to Philadelphia. There's no buses, no taxis, no trains. How do we get back to the U.S.?"

"That's up to you, sorry."

Seymour and Ailish took a harried taxi to the local Walmart where they could finally phone their daughter in Philadelphia.

Seymour held the phone away from his face, shocked when Margaret told him, "Dad, I'm sorry. I have to go to New York. Please, find a way home if you can."

Ailish seized the receiver from Seymour. "What's the matter, Maggie? Your father's turning white as a sheet."

"Oh, Mom. It's Sean."

"Sean? What's wrong with my grandson?"

"Got a phone call from Sean's wife. Sean's been admitted to a psyche ward. He was working the scene at the twin towers. They say he's gone crazy. Jean's got the baby, she's got no way to get into the city. You'll have to find your own way home."

Seymour grabbed the phone. "There *is* no way back, Godammit."

"Maybe, a taxi? Sorry, Dad, I have to go."

"It's 500 miles, just to Bangor, Maine."

"Dad, my son is in a New York hospital. Call me later."

"Where?"

"Check the New York Fire Department. Bye."

*

Twenty-four years had passed after Margaret Abramson McMillan nearly lost Sean in childbirth. Doctors said she would never have more children, so she and husband, Patrick, decided to adopt, raising a baby girl into a beautiful 21 year-old model named Naomi. Seymour and Ailish were doting grandparents, attending every milestone, baby sitting, taking Sean and Naomi to theme parks, zoos, beaches and parties. Now that the grandkids were adults, Seymour and Ailish went about following their dreams of traveling around the world, while still able.

It was hard for Margaret, a divorcee, to turn her back on her parents at a time of need, but her son needed her more. She had to get to New York. She had to be with her boy.

The clouds exploded into a rainstorm as Margaret embarked on her drive north on I-95. She used her cell phone to call Sean's wife. "Tell me more, Wanda. What happened to my son?"

"Don't know, one of the firefighters said he lost control when a body fell from the twin towers. He's been catatonic ever since."

The conversation continued another fifteen minutes as Margaret sped north, squinting to see through the smearing raindrops. Suddenly, taillights sparkled before her. Traffic had come to halt, but Margaret could not stop in time. The phone flew from her hand as she slammed the brakes, ramming the SUV in front of her. As the air bag inflated, she heard another strident screech of brakes from behind. She looked into the rear view mirror and saw an eighteen-wheeler jacknife sideways, rambling toward her like a derailed freight train.

*

<u>Forest Hills, Queens, New York</u>

At 8:25 a.m., big Gus Machinski, real estate magnate, had just settled a deal with a Japanese developer which would boost his sales receipts for the year into the tens of millions. So excited was he, that he offered to buy everyone in the office dinner at the local steak restaurant that evening. But first, he had to deliver the final contracts signed in blue-ink to the firm representing the sellers. No Faxes.

Gus called the courier service but they weren't available until the afternoon. He'd ask his secretary if she'd bring the papers into the city, but she was taking the morning off. Other sales personnel were busy with clients. Gus didn't want to make the trip himself, so he offered three hundred dollars to a woman he knew in the next door graphics design office if she would deliver the documents for him. "Would you mind? These are important, they must get in their hands this morning."

"Three hundred bucks? Sure thing, Gus. Wow. Thanks a lot."

*

Ailish Abramson had her hands full. Seymour felt sickly which worried her deeply. They were trapped in Moncton with no way to get out. Finally she had an idea. "How much cash do you have, Seymour?"

"I don't know."

"Well, look."

Seymour opened his wallet and found ninety dollars in tens and fives, but he had some more bills stashed away in a secret compartment. "Looks like we have about five hundred dollars. But we still have credit cards."

"Credit cards won't help us, Seymour. We'll hire someone, that's all."

"Hire what? Who?"

"We'll pay someone cash to drive us to Bangor, Maine. Then we'll rent a car."

"Well, okay."

Two hours later, they were in the back seat of a Toyota Corolla being driven by an assistant manager of Walmart who would take the rest of the day off sick to earn four hundred American dollars for driving two elderly Americans into Maine. The ride would entail eight hours, mostly on desolate roads. Along the way, Seymour leaned his weary head back to rest. Ailish took his hand and watched the landscape pass by. Any joy they could have savored from their trip to Europe was now irrelevant. Thoughts of her grandson, Sean, and his children, and Margaret raced through her mind, wishing she could be there to comfort everyone.

She looked over at dozing Seymour with reverence and pictured their twin daughters, Margaret and Marianne, now fifty years old, her own sister in New Jersey, her toy Poodle and her Siamese cat. She nudged her husband. "Wake up, Seymour. We're coming up on the border. Customs." She nudged him again. And, again. And, again.

"Oh, dear — "

*

EPILOGUE

People often lose perspective at the sound of statistics because mass losses become numbers, not human beings. Not only did the terrorists murder 2,977 innocent human beings that day, it is impossible to calculate the collateral injuries, post traumatic disorders, motherless and fatherless kids, and other related deaths that stemmed from that fateful morning. This story was about those who didn't make the news, nor add to the statistics, nor seemed to matter. But they do matter. They are victims of the attack on America as much as those who perished in the inferno.

*

The stress conquered old Seymour Abramson before he ever reached Bangor. He died peacefully while napping in the back seat of the Canadian's Toyota as his devoted Irish wife of fifty-three years held his hand.

*

Their daughter, Margaret Abramson McMillan never made it to her son's side at the hospital in Manhattan. She was killed instantly when an eighteen-wheeler slammed into the rear of her car on I-95.

*

Sean Michael McMillan served as a New York City firefighter for only two months. By the time his wife arrived at the hospital he was under sedation, barely able to speak. She grabbed his hand and held it tightly. "Oh, Sean, I love you. You're going to be okay."

He struggle to answer, lips quivering. "Aunt...Aunt Mary...Ohhh..."

"What about Aunt Mary?"

He looked way and squeezed his eyes shut.

Sean became one of the estimated 422,000 people who would suffer with Post Traumatic Stress for the rest of his life as a result of the attack on 9/11.

*

Firefighter Jose Raul Campos was supposed to remain at street level manning the hose at the base of the twin towers. But when Sean McMillan had to be hospitalized, the Fire supervisor reassigned Jose to rescue duties inside the building. Thus, Jose became one of the 343 firefighters killed that day when the building collapsed, leaving two small children without a father.

*

Then, there was that name: Marianne Lynn Abramson Ormond. She was a graphic designer in Queens, New York, married with three grown kids and two grandchildren. Sadly, Marianne was tempted by the lure of a fast three hundred dollars offered to her by Gus Machinski for delivering a large envelope to the 92nd floor of the World Trade Center.

Kawhack! Kaplop!

"Aunt...Aunt Mary...Ohhh..."

Sean gasped at the sight of that twisted body whose face rested upward on the street. Her name was Marianne Lynn Abramson Ormond. She was also his mother's twin sister.

*

Ailish Abramson lost both daughters and her husband in a single day, in three different places, all connected by the same dots. Her life would never be the same.

Ripple effect.

The Good Old Days

"You know you're getting old when everything
hurts. And what doesn't hurt, doesn't work."
— Hy Gardner

"K-K-K-Katieee, beautiful Katieee, you're the only g-g-g-girl that
I adore...."

"Sing it, Wally!"

"Nothin' could be finer than to be in Carolina in the
moooornin'...."

"All right!"

"Wally, do you know, *The Girl That I Marry?*"

The little man changed key without skipping a beat. *"...*
will have to be, as soft and as pink as a nurseryyy... Of course,
I know all those songs."

It was a typical Saturday afternoon at the Woodcrest
Nursing Home, perched high atop the tallest peak
overlooking idyllic Maggie Valley, North Carolina. Everyone
had gathered in the recreation room to hear Wally at the
antique baby grand, playing his usual renditions of old tunes,
generating an explosion of nostalgia for twenty-five fellow
geriatrics.

*"Frankie and Johnnie were lovers...*Yeah! *Oh lordie how they*
could love..." Come on, everybody sing along."

A few attempted to join in. Some sat in wheelchairs,

tilted awry, white heads bobbing, gnarled fingers tapping to the lively rhythms. A collection of wonderful memories seemed to linger through their minds, bringing a sparkle to their eyes and an upward curl to their lips.

"You must remember this, a kiss is just a kiss..."

Once a day, in the late afternoon, Walter Samuel Mahoney would entertain, just as he had in the old vaudeville days, and in piano bars where crowds packed the Queen's Terrace nightclub in New York City. He loved seeing traces of smiles on those elderly faces, as though they were a mirror of his own. It was the one time of the day he wasn't lonely.

"Time's up," barked the tall skinny woman in a white smock. He checked the cockeyed wall clock and saw it was after five. All the wheelchairs turned around and rolled away, almost in unison.

Other than diabetes, skin cancer, and arthritic knees, Wally's biggest problem was his mouth. He was a chronic chatterbox, always rambling about the good old days, reminiscing about past entertainers and the by-gone loves of his life. Everyone avoided him like the plague, except when he played music.

One crisp autumn morning, Wally was sitting on the front porch of the old converted manor when a van pulled into the curved driveway. It was an ordinary scene at Crestwood, a frail elderly woman being lifted into her wheelchair then rolled inside the huge oaken doors. He studied her as she passed by, head covered with a bandana, eyes dulled but as large as saucers, skin flaccid, face sagging.

"What is her name?" Wally asked the attendant.

"That's Mrs. Van Horn." The attendant pointed to his head. "Alzheimer's."

"Oh. Sorry."

The next morning, he trapped the new resident in the park and began bombarding her with his stories. She sat hunched, seemingly indifferent, gazing out into space. Wally had finally found someone who would listen to his ramblings.

Every day after the break of dawn, Wally volunteered to wheel Mrs. Van Horn to the wooden bench overlooking the valley where they fed squirrels, marveled at the views, and talked. Well, Wally talked. And talked. She was a living death, fixated on the clouds, showing an occasional glimmer of life with her faint, toothless smile.

Wally babbled on about sharing a stage with such greats as Burns and Allen, Milton Berle and Rudy Vallee. She didn't understand a word he was saying, but, at least she didn't roll away. He had a captive audience, at last.

"Ah, Mrs. Van Horn, you should have been there. The audiences loved me. Every time I played a song, they asked for more. When the show was over, I couldn't get off the stage. Sophie Tucker called me the best songster since Irving Berlin.

"Those were the days, yes siree. My name appeared on a marquis along with Tommy Dorsey. Pretty good, huh? And when I played the Queen's Terrace nightclub, the mob wouldn't let them hire any other piano player but me.

"The damn war screwed everything up. I was heading for stardom. Roosevelt coulda held out, but, who knows? The war did more than screw up my career. It ripped my heart out.

"Three and a half years in a Japanese prison camp. Never thought I'd ever see freedom again. I nearly starved to death by the time MacArthur arrived. Weighed just over sixty pounds.

"I thought Kate would have waited. Yeah, I know. She thought I was dead. Ah, things happen. I came home, and found out she had married some other joker, a lawyer. I lost her. God, I adored that woman. I'll never forget how

I dreamed of her during those years, imagining the day I'd come home to her arms, her sweet smelling hair, those wonderful green eyes that looked at me like I was the only man alive, her hero. I was her hero. Ha. Imagine that?

"Ah, well, so I married Sylvia. Had two kids. Boys. She was a good woman. Together forty-two years. They're all dead now. It's bad enough to outlive your wife, but to outlive your own kids, that's pretty sad, eh?" He looked into the old woman's gaze and gave conversation a try. "You got any kids, Mrs. Van Horn?"

Her saucer eyes shifted toward his for a brief moment, then turned away as though he were talking in a foreign tongue.

"Sorry, didn't mean to pry. Look, I appreciate you listening to me. These old farts around here say I talk too much. Maybe that's true, but they sure like my music. I'd play all day if they'd let me. God, I hate being old. Don't you?

"Before the war, Kate and me, we were a team. We did comedy, songs, and impersonations. Audiences loved us. Kate was the real act, not me. She had magic on the stage, like she could reach out and touch everyone's hearts. She made them laugh, made them cry. She did Bette Davis, 'Petah, Petah, Petah,' like no one else, and when she imitated Garbo, heh heh, she would lower her voice, raise her arms and say, 'I vant to be alone!'

"I never felt the same excitement from Sylvia like I felt from her. Kate was pure magic. We were always touching, Kate and I. We'd walk holding hands, she'd wrap her arms around me at the movies. Wow, the feel of her hand against my face..."

Wally hesitated, reflecting on the days when life was perfect, eyes flitting about. He blinked to avoid a tear from showing.

"Heh. She'd take my pinky finger, you know, and link it

with hers, even when we sat at the dinner table. All the time. She said she wanted to always stay connected. Sometimes, I'd wake up in the morning and her pinky was linked up to my pinky, completely asleep. Amazing, huh?"

Wally's eyes started to well up as he paused, savoring those precious moments in time. As always, Mrs. Van Horn remained motionless, staring out over the mountain tops where an array of brilliant colors — gold, auburn and red — painted the rolling landscape.

Wally's voice turned sullen as he looked back at the old manor. "This place is like a living coffin. I ain't ready to die yet. Uh uh. There's more to do yet in my life. Know what I mean?" He stared over the horizon, dropped both hands on his lap and whispered, "Nope. I'm not ready. Not yet."

Wally leaned over and patted the old woman on her hand. "Hey, thanks for listening. Sorry if I get carried away." He looked at his watch and saw it was nearly time for his daily show.

Wally stood and turned Mrs. Van Horn's chair around and began pushing her toward the manor. As they neared the doors, he heard an strange guttural sound from the direction of her chair. Suddenly, she lifted her hand into mid air.Curious now, he stopped and stepped to her front. During a long and quiet pause, he leaned over and peered deep into her soul. That's when she ended her blank stare and looked directly at him. She sucked a labored breath, opened her toothless mouth, tilted her head back and extended her quivering hand to his. He allowed her the gesture and watched in astonishment as she spoke not a word. Her mouth opened wide, like she was trying to talk, but could not. Then, with both hands trembling, she grabbed his right hand and in a sudden jerk, locked her pinky finger around his own.

Like static electricity, hair rose on Wally's arms. Astonished, gasping, he leaned closer. He peered deep into her eyes and saw a dull green. Then he gently lifted her wrist to read the I.D. bracelet: *Katherine Van Horn*. For a fleeting moment, he saw the hint of sparkle in her eye. Then, she drifted off once more.

Wally's eyes welled into pools of utter joy. *Oh, my Kate. My Kate. I don't believe... You've come back to me.* He looked around the manicured lawn and saw no one. He let the tears flow, kneeling before her, his head in her lap, weeping uncontrollably, sensing the quiver of her hand upon his head.

Wally snuck into Kate's room that night, so they could sleep together, fulfilling a lifelong dream. Sometime during the early morning hours, he awoke to the sensation that Katherine had stopped breathing. She had been cuddled to his underbelly, pinkies linked, rigid. For the next three hours, he refused to let go until attendants pried his finger away.

Wally had lost his greatest love, but he was the happiest man on earth.

Truth-o-meter: 40%

The Power of Love

> *"If you've never been hated by your child,*
> *you've never been a parent."*
> — Bette Davis

"Why, Son?" asked the portly plain-clothed cop.

"I don't know."

He offered a tissue. "Come on, eleven-year-old boys don't cry."

"I'm sorry." The boy lowered his face into his hands, weeping.

"Easy, Son. Take your time. Tell me what happened."

The boy saw a mirrored wall on one side of the tiny room and figured there were people watching from behind, just like on TV. "Is there anyone in there?"

"Would you feel better if we went somewhere else?" The boy nodded. "Come. We'll go and get a burger. How's that?"

"Okay."

*

Two Months Earlier

Aaron Michael Feinstein shared a table with his weekend father at the Olive Garden in Columbia, South Carolina, just like most Saturdays at lunch. And, just like almost every Saturday, his father opened a laptop, lay it on the table then handed the boy a spare iPhone with which to play video games. Aaron could order anything he wanted on the menu, could call any friend on the phone, or play any game. What he didn't have was the company of his father. But, that was normal.

As Aaron dived into his meatballs and penne pasta, he watched his father talk and eat at the same time, holding a phone to his ear while chomping antipasto. He could tell by the sheepish look on his father's face that he was talking to a woman. A jealous moment, indeed. Aaron wondered how it would feel to be on the receiving end of all that attention. He wanted to tell his dad why he was giving up cello lessons at school and that his grades were going down to C's and D's, but he figured his father had more important things to think about.

Aaron's parents had been divorced two years. But they lived like they were divorced while still married. No one ever talked nice to each other. His father had always tended to business, morning, noon and night. Their house along the banks of idyllic Lake Murray was like a mausoleum: high ceilings, big walls, extravagant art, large windows, stone stairways and the perennial echo of voices and heavy metal rock music.

He saw more of the maids and gardeners than he did his mother and father combined. His mother was an elegant lady. She owned a chain of beauty shops in Columbia, Charleston and Greenville. Many people worked for her, including stock brokers and accountants. Men often came to the house to take her out. Some owned large boats and private airplanes. She wore fancy dresses that revealed her ample bosom.

Aaron thought about her a lot, remembering when he was a small kid how she stroked his hair every night before putting him to sleep, telling him stories, softly singing songs, smiling, caring. He wondered what happened?

"Hey, Champ, check out the desserts. They got carrot cake and ice cream," his father said, craning to look at him over the laptop.

"Oh. Yeah. Okay, I guess."

"What's the matter, Champ?"

"Nothin'."

"Okay. Look, I got one more call to make, then we'll go to the movies, okay?"

"Yeah, sure."

An hour later, Aaron found himself sitting in a stadium seat through an animated movie while Dad got lost somewhere in the lobby or the bathroom. When the movie was over, his father drove him home. "Okay, Champ. See you next week."

"Yeah, okay."

*

"Aaron, your supper is in the microwave."

"Okay, Mom."

"Aaron, put the video game down a minute and open your door."

Aaron ignored his mother and continued his make-believe war against the Titans, sound effects included.

"Aaron, did you hear me?"

"I can't. I'm naked."

"Why are you naked?"

"Cause that's how you have to fight the Titans."

"Oh, Aaron. Look, Mommy's got to go out. I'll be back in a little while."

"Bye, Mom."

"Keep the doors locked. Don't open the door for any strangers."

"Bye, Mom."

Aaron waited five minutes until he knew for sure he was all alone, then logged on to the computer where he monitored chat rooms just to see what people were saying to each other, especially the girls. He knew the TV dinner was in the kitchen, but he'd wait a while. Before long, he was into a chat with some girl who said her name was Boobigoo. He pretended to be eighteen and called himself Whopperman. The chat was all lies, each telling of wonders they could do, people who they weren't, exploits that never existed. Just another evening in Aaron's dull, listless life, waiting for stimulation that was non-existent and attention that came only from fantasy gleaned from an electronic machine.

Yet, Aaron had it all; a three-hundred square foot bedroom overlooking the lake complete with surround sound for the plasma television set, iPod, computers, bicycles, electric guitars, trips to camp in summer and a closet full of expensive clothing he hardly ever wore. His parents were very generous, giving him everything and anything, except themselves.

Finally, Aaron got hungry and gobbled up a Stouffer's family-sized platter of spaghetti and meatballs as he watched cartoons on the living room television. Bored, tired of electronic games, he called his only friend.

"Hey, Chad. What's up?"

"Hey, Man."

After six words between them, they had nothing more to say. Aaron finally broke the ice. "Well, I just thought I'd see what was happening."

"Aaron, what's the matter with you, anyway?"

"What do you mean?"

"First, you don't show up at the basketball court yesterday

afternoon. You drop out of orchestra. You don't talk to no one. You all right, Man?"

"Yeah. I'm okay. My mom's out. Again."

"Yeah, so?"

"She's always out."

"Why don't you go and live with your father?"

"My father's too busy. Besides, he's with that new chick. He don't want me around."

"Hey, Man. I gotta go."

"Wait, Chad. Can I ask you a question?"

"Sure, what's up?"

"I'm gonna take off. Don't tell nobody, okay?"

"What do you mean?"

"Going away. Wanna come with me?"

"Where are you going?"

"I don't know, for sure. Maybe Orlando. Disney World."

"Orlando? Aaron, you're just eleven years old. How are you going to eat?"

"I have some money saved. How bout it? Come with me?"

"No way. Why would I run away? Look Man, you got everything. Your parents are rich. The other kids would do anything to have all your stuff."

"I ain't got friends."

"I'm your friend."

"Yeah, I know. Everyone thinks I'm a nerd."

Chad laughed aloud into the phone. "That's cause you act like a nerd, Aaron. Come on. Let's you, me, and my friends all go to the mall tomorrow tonight."

"No. I'm leaving."

"Aaron?"

*

"Hey, boy. Wake up."

"Huh?"

"Boy, it's seven in the morning. You been asleep all night."

Aaron stirred and rubbed his eyes, then looked out the bus window and saw people walking to and fro, wheeling suitcases along the sidewalk. A thin black man in a blue uniform leaned over him with a concerned look on his face. Aaron asked, "Uh, where am I?"

"You're in Melbourne. Florida. You got parents, or anyone meeting you here?

As consciousness set it, Aaron realized he was in a Greyhound bus. "I'm supposed to be in Orlando."

"Then you on the wrong bus, Boy. Or, you missed your transfer. Come on to the station, we'll call your mama or your daddy."

They were words Aaron didn't want to hear. "That's okay. I'll be fine."

The driver helped him to the luggage bin where he retrieved his pillowcase full of clothes, maps and a small laptop. "You sure I can't call your mama, or someone?"

"Uh, I'm okay. I know where to go, I just need a taxi."

"You sure, Boy?"

Outside the Melbourne International Airport, which also serves as a bus terminal, Aaron walked to a parked cab. When he entered, the driver asked, "Where to, young fella?"

"I don't know."

The driver turned around. "What do you mean, you don't know?"

"Can you take me to Disney World?"

"Too far. You're talking almost two hundred miles round trip."

"Is there a beach? I want to go to the beach."

"Are you lost, Son?"

"No. No. I just want to see the beach."

"Any beach?"

"Yeah."

"You got the money?"

Aaron pulled out a wad of cash and held it up. "I got money,"

The driver could have easily driven the boy across the Melbourne Causeway, a distance of four miles, for a fare of less than four dollars. Instead, he drove Aaron the long way up Interstate 95, to Cocoa, Florida, then east to the world famous surfing Mecca of Cocoa Beach, totaling thirty-three miles and a forty-two dollar fare.

"Drop me at Denny's restaurant, please. Over there."

For the next two weeks, Aaron slept on the beaches, surviving on fast-food burgers and fries, wandering from place to place along Highway A1A, stopping often at Ron Jon's Beach Store where he bought a cool pair of sunglasses, wild tee shirts and a large towel to sleep on. He enjoyed all this time to himself, looking in dressing room mirrors, changing his blond hair from hanging down his neck, to spikes with gel, wild, crazy, free. He especially enjoyed the busy pier where bigger kids played volley ball on the beach and surfers rode the waves when the water was rough. The girls were beautiful, every one of them, and they all wore skimpy bathing suits.

But his money was running out and he had no other source. He wondered if his mother missed him very much, if he'd gotten even with her for ignoring him all these months and years. Maybe she didn't care that he ran away. Maybe she was glad. Either way, his father wouldn't have to be bothered with him on Saturdays.

Someone told him to check Historic Downtown Cocoa Village, so he took a bus the five miles to the mainland.

There, quaint village streets were lined with boutiques and cafes, and a theater where they held live performances of Broadway shows. He wondered if they'd pay him to sing.

Night had fallen. His money was all spent. Aaron was now penniless. On Friday evening, many people were attending the theater. He stood outside wearing his dirty sneakers, wrinkled jeans and a new Ron Jon tee shirt, gawking at the well-dressed theater goers. One elderly lady stopped and patted him in the head. "What a nice boy."

In a surprise impulse, he asked, "Do you have a little money, please? So I can get something to eat?"

"Why, what a shame," she said. "Here's five dollars."

"Thanks."

He barely heard her asking, "Where are your parents?" He was already running down the street and out of sight. That night, he slept next to River Front park under the causeway bridge that spanned the Indian River. Fortunately, there were public bathrooms available with the doors unlocked.

Aaron was in trouble now. He didn't want to call his mother or father, because it would be embarrassing to show that he was too weak to survive on his own. He also didn't want to be a bother.

The morning sun had risen over the horizon as he sat on a concrete bench eating scraps from his pizza from the night before. Seagulls flew overhead, squawking. A boat pulled out from the docks. All was quiet on this summer morning. A woman with a scarf on her head walked over and sat beside him.

"Hello," she said.

"Hello."

"Are you lost?"

"No."

"What's your name?"

Aaron dared not give his real name. "Uh. John. Johnny."

"Hi Johnny. I'm Madeline."

"Hello." *Why is she asking me questions?*

She had an endearing smile and a glint in her eye. From her large, cloth bag, she pulled out a package wrapped in foil. "Egg salad sandwich. You want part of it?"

Aaron felt his stomach growl. "Okay. Thanks."

Something about this woman was warm and comforting. He hoped she would stay around a while. As he started munching on the sandwich, he was startled by a tap on his shoulder from behind. "Hey, Son. We need to talk to you," said a deep masculine voice.

Aaron looked up and saw two uniformed police officers, one a female, the other a giant white man. "What did I do?" Aaron asked, his heart pounding.

"We have reports that a small boy has been hanging around here all alone for a couple days, panhandling. Is that you? Are you lost, boy?"

"No."

"You run away from somewhere?"

"No."

"What's your name?"

"Johnny."

"What's your last name?"

"Uh. Johnson."

"Johnny Johnson, huh? You better come with us."

As Aaron started to his feet, the woman named Madeline spoke up. "Officer, Johnny here, is with me. I'm his nanny."

"Are you sure, Ma'am?"

"Yes, Officers. Thank very much. The boy is just fine, well taken care of." She took Aaron's hand. "Come, Johnny, time to go home."

*

Aaron was greeted by a tiny Yorkshire Terrier the moment he entered the double-wide trailer. "Wow, what's his name?"

"Toy Boy."

"Cool name. He's licking me all over. Wow. Neat dog."

"Come, Johnny, I'll make you some cocoa, and cereal. You like Fruit Loops?"

"Yeah. Okay."

The tiny living room was neat and tidy, with two chairs and couch and a small television set. He hadn't watched TV in three weeks and realized he didn't miss it very much. Framed photographs lined the end tables, mostly of a woman with a man, and others of a small boy. She lay the bowl of cereal on the counter, a plate with toast for herself, and a cup of tea. "Come on, you're hungry. You can tell me all about your journey, okay?"

His instincts suggested he ought to keep his mouth shut, but there was something about her that he trusted. The cereal was delicious, especially with bananas on top. He hadn't eaten that well in a long time. The woman seemed to be content to share the table. She was a quiet lady, always smiling with a glint in her eye. "Tell me, Johnny, where do you live?"

"I used to live in Columbia. That's in South Carolina."

"Used to, huh? And where do you live now?"

He shrugged. "Around."

How long have you been away from home?"

"Three weeks, and three days."

"I see."

A thought occurred. "Are you going to send me back?"

She smiled broadly as she readjusted her head scarf. "Not unless you want to go back."

That was a relief. Now he felt even more trusting. "My mother and father don't like me very much. I'm a boring kid."

"Really? I don't think you're boring."

"You don't?"

"No. I've never seen Toy Boy get so excited over a child before."

"Really?"

"Really."

"Can I stay with you for a couple days?"

"Sure. When was the last time you slept in a bed?"

"Three weeks..."

"...and three days. Right?"

"Yeah."

She sipped on her mug then looked Aaron directly in the eyes. "Can I tell you a little story?"

Aaron wondered what this was all about. "Story?"

"Johnny, I lost a son. His name was Johnny too, just like you. He was nine years old. You remind me very much of him. He was a polite child. You even laugh like him."

"What happened to him?"

"He died."

The answer stunned Aaron. "Uh. I'm sorry. How?"

"He had leukemia. Many years ago. 1989."

"Oh. Is that his picture over there?"

"Yes." Madeline paused a moment, then invited Aaron to come to the living room. "Johnny and I used to play cards. Do you like cards?"

"Never played cards."

"Do you play any games with your mom or dad?"

Aaron told her about his uninspiring home life, rife with boredom, fractured parents and electronic baby sitters. "We never play anything. I'm like a cat or a dog. They feed me and take me to the vet, then I take care of myself the rest of the time."

She looked at Aaron endearingly. "Come. Sit next to me."

Aaron wondered what she had in mind, but he still trusted her, so he moved over, cautious. "Okay."

She put her arm around him. He felt like melted butter in her bosom. "You're a good boy, I can see that." Aaron wanted to cry, but he had never seen men cry, only his mother and other girls in the movies. So he remained still. "You stay here with me. I'll take care of you. But you must know something first."

"What's that?"

"I'm not well. I have to go to the doctor every three days for treatment. You can come with me if you want."

"Okay."

"I don't have any other family that's living. My husband passed away ten years ago."

"Oh. I'm sorry."

"Sometimes, a nurse comes over to take care of me. She gives me therapy and medicine."

"I'll help take care of you."

The woman smiled broadly and hugged him close. "You're a good boy. We'll have a nice time together."

Immediately drawn to the woman's affection, Aaron felt a pang of guilt which led to a confession. "I, uh, have to tell you something. I lied."

"Oh? About what?"

"My name. My name is really Aaron. Not Johnny."

"That's okay. I'll still call you Johnny, if you don't mind. Is that okay?"

"Sure."

Toy Boy jumped onto the couch and sat on Aaron's lap. Madeline lay her head back with a smile on her face, kissed the boy on his forehead, then removed her scarf. Aaron had never seen a bald-headed woman before.

*

Aaron now lived in a home, not a house. Madeline had health problems, but she did her best to make breakfasts and dinners on the days she was home. When she felt strong, she took Aaron on day trips to the Brevard County Zoo, the Kennedy Space Center, the air boat rides and lots of movies. Sometimes she just waited on a bench while Aaron went on rides and looked at sights. Every night, they played games like Twenty Questions, Trivial Pursuit, Monopoly, cards and backgammon. She also helped him with sixth grade English and math, reminding him that he had to go back to school one day and do his very best.

She told Aaron about her own life growing up in the poor neighborhoods of Mobile, Alabama, and how she remembered being a little girl who wasn't allowed to use the same water fountains, swim in the same pools, or go to the same schools as white children. But she had the will and determination to overcome rejection and hardship, and went on to college where she earned a degree and became a school teacher.

She implored Aaron to always see the bright side of life, that all those hardships were meant to teach him how to overcome, because life would was certain to be a journey of overcoming obstacles. She told the boy that she was sure his mother loved him, but that she had lost her way for a little while and to be patient, for she would find her way again and they would be happy.

He listened closely to her stories because he knew she cared from the bottom of her heart. She didn't worry about her image, or about money and material things. She cared about loving others and showing the way, if she could. Aaron knew he meant a lot to her and he did his best to attend to her needs, washing the dishes, cleaning the bathrooms, and taking care of Toy Boy, his favorite dog of all time.

Eventually, the day trips ended. They played games less often. Now it was he who had to make breakfasts and dinners, because Madeline was feeling ill. She stopped going to treatments three days a week, and she lay in bed most of the day. He sat on the folding chair next to her bed, leaned forward with his elbows on the bed and asked her to tell him more stories. She patted him on the head, and whispered, "You know, Johnny. I should have made you go home. I was wrong to keep you here."

Aaron felt a pang in his heart. "No. Oh, no. I want to be here with you."

"Someday, I won't be able to play games with you any more. You have to be strong, okay? You can't choose your family, but you must make the best of it, because it's your life — not their life — you have to lead."

A moment of warmth overwhelmed the boy. "Can I tell you something, Madeline?"

"Sure. What is it?"

"I ... I love you."

"Oh, dear."

The boy began to weep. "I love you so much. I don't ever want to leave you."

"I love you too. You're a good boy."

"Promise me..."

"I can't make promises, Johnny. Because then, I might break a promise I couldn't keep."

The days and nights passed slowly as Madeline remained in her bed most of the time. A nurse visited now and then to make sure she had medicine and her private needs, but

Aaron found himself back to watching TV and playing with his computer games more and more to pass the time.

On a rainy Sunday night, Aaron turned off the TV to get ready for bed, when he heard a grunting sound come from Madeline's room. When he entered, he saw her lying on her back with the night lamp still on. The room stank of a rancid odor. Her face was sallow, eyes sunken, her body a mere skeleton with skin wrapped around the bones, and she had no hair. She lifted her hand weakly and motioned for him to come closer.

He sat on the folding chair and leaned forward with his elbows on the bed. "Are you okay?" he asked, holding her hand.

She turned her head slowly to see the love in his eyes. "You're...a...good...boy...Aaron."

It was the first time she ever called him by his real name and it warmed Aaron's heart. As the tears rolled down his cheek, she faced the boy with dull, haggard eyes, then drew a faint smile that seemed to remain on her face. He continued holding her hand while she continued looking at him with that smile. When he moved, left or right, her eyes remained fixed. That's when Aaron knew.

Alone in a small bedroom filled with death, disease and love, with a small dog by his chair, Aaron Michael Feinstein bawled aloud. "Please, no. I love you! Please, I love you!"

*

As Aaron finished his burger and fries at McDonald's, the plain-clothed cop answered his ringing cell phone. He could see the officer was talking about him, because he kept glancing his way. Then he heard the officer say, "Oh, she's in Melbourne now? Tell her to come to the station."

Aaron asked, "Is that my mom?"

The cop furrowed his brow, "Yes, Son. You're gonna have to go home with your mama. You know that."

"I know. It's okay."

"You really put your family through an ordeal. Everyone thought you were kidnapped or dead."

Aaron's first response was to say he was sorry, but then he realized that he wasn't. He was glad he ran away, no matter what happened. He had discovered the difference between love of humanity and love of things. And, if his mother or father could not provide the love he felt from the woman named Madeline, he knew there was a world of Madelines out there, and his life could be filled with love.

"Can I ask a question?"

"What's that?"

"What's happening to Toy Boy?"

"With what?"

"Her little dog."

"Oh, they took it to the rescue shelter."

"Can I have it?"

"You better ask you mother, not me."

Aaron was left alone in the little square room for over an hour with nothing to do but think. He had no idea how she was going to react, but he hoped she had at least missed him. If she was mad, that would be okay, because it meant that she cared. At the sound of the door latch, his heart jumped into his throat.

"Oh, Aaron, my Aaron, are you all right?"

"I'm fine, Mom."

She rushed to him, weeping, wiping tears, grateful that he was not harmed. And that made him feel very good. "Aaron, I'm so sorry."

"What are you sorry for? I'm the one who ran away."

"No, Son. It was me who has been running away. And I promise I'll never run away again."

She brought him close to her bosom and hugged him, and told him how much she loved him. "I love you too, Mom."

"Come, Aaron, let's go home."

"Before we go home, can we go to a funeral? It's tomorrow, in Cocoa."

"Huh?"

"It's just an old woman. We were friends. I'll tell you all about her. I promise."

"Well, I suppose so. Whatever you want."

Aaron returned to his home on Lake Murray in Columbia where he resumed lessons on the cello, made straight A's in school, had the undivided love and attention from his mom and the daily companionship of Toy Boy, his favorite dog of all time. Throughout his life, he would never forget the power of love he learned from a sick old lady named Madeline who changed his world and gave him strength to overcome any adversity.

She was right, after all.

And they all lived happily ever after.

A Flat (Ulent) Experience

"He couldn't ad lib a fart after a baked-bean dinner."
— Johnny Carson

Police Commander, Burt Ackerman, passed gas in an elevator.

End of story? Not quite.

He thought it a safe venture, for he was all alone. He had been holding the giant bowel bubble, it seemed, for more than half an hour. Finally, the relief was incredible, like a balloon overinflated before all the air is released. Ahhh. God is good, indeed.

It all started with a trip to the 29th floor of the government center building in Miami, where Burt attended a meeting of high level mucky-mucks in starched shirts, paisley ties, and wing-tipped shoes. Such settings always unnerved Burt. He hated being around stuffy people consumed with self-importance. He'd much rather be sitting at his office, or better yet, in front of a wide screen plasma television watching his favorite football team beating the tar out of their opponent. Better yet, telling stories to his little granddaughter while she sat upon his lap. But work was work, which meant multi-tasking at the desk, handling phone complaints, trouble-shooting with dissatisfied cops, budget problems, avalanches of paperwork and a pile of "urgent" messages from one boss or another. Oy.

Business lunches were the death of him, always at the same old restaurants. That pasta fagioli at Paladin's Trattoria did it every time. It seemed to cook like a pot of hot chili until it reached the boiling point. He just could not keep it inside.

The meeting was another boring waste of time. An attractive secretary in a svelte business suit and red stilettos kept coming in and out of the meeting room to deliver papers and messages to the Assistant County Manager as he chaired the meeting. Burt's eyeballs were glued to her every step, every gesture, every moment in the room. He imagined her pulling the pin from her French twist coif and that auburn red hair falling to her shoulders. He caught the waft of her perfume each time she passed by. About thirty, she had chiseled features, with an Elizabeth Taylor nose, the slanted eyes of Sophia Loren and the cockiness of Katherine Hepburn. He pretended to be tuned into the meeting, faking it well, but his fantasies overwhelmed any sense of duty. Each time she left the room, he waited anxiously for her return. Each time, he could feel the skip in his heartbeat.

Wow, what is she doing here? She should be walking the super model runway or auditioning at MGM.

He heard the manager call her on the intercom: "Denise, would you please bring me the Johnson folder."

Denise. Ah yes, good name. Very female. Can't get that mixed up with cross-gender names, like Dale, or Niki. He remembered a gorgeous French movie star in the 1950s named Denise Darcel.

Halfway through the meeting, the pasta fagiolo began its internal churning process. He knew he would have to leave the room soon if the meeting continued. It was destined for Shock and Awe! One of those ear-shattering boomers, the kind that startle and make folks gasp. They'd look the other way while holding their noses and desperately pretending they didn't hear a thing.

Finally, the meeting ended. Passing by, he expected to see Denise at the secretary's desk but she was nowhere in sight. He headed for the bank of elevators, glad to see that no one was around. But there came the numbers cruncher, George McGirk, a government accountant who corralled Burt outside the elevators, bending his ear about inane problems with freezing employee vacancies. His brain cried out,"*Get away from me, George. I have to FART!*"

George walked off, pad in hand. Relief was now in sight as he headed for the elevators and pushed the 'down' button. He paced the floor anxiously hoping to remain alone. The pearly gates opened. He was sooo happy. Two businessmen exited as Burt hurriedly entered the mirrored cab and pushed the button to the fourth Floor.

When the doors closed, it felt like an out-of-body experience. It sounded more like an IED that exploded in the streets of Baghdad. The cab shook, mirrors clouded. He worried that the elevator might crash between floors from the shock. Well, it all seemed that way.

Relief is a cold drink when you're thirsty. Relief is making up when you argue with your spouse. This wasn't just relief. This was worth praising the Lord.

Burt leaned back against the rail in his solitude as the elevator started its descent. He caught the putrid scent the same moment he felt the elevator slow to a stop at the 26th floor. A malodorous pall hung heavily like fresh sludge from a sewer, enveloping the entire elevator cabin, reeking, stinking. He felt his eyeballs burn. There was nowhere to run.

The elevator stopped. The doors slid open. His heart plunged. *Oh no! Red Stilettos?* Beautiful Denise stood, file folders in hand, waiting, smiling. His heart raced. "Well, hello," she said as she stepped inside.

This was like being naked on the fifty yard line in the middle of Super Bowl halftime. No. Worse.

His instinct was to run, but it was too late. The doors were closing and *she* was inside, just her — and Burt. No escape.

"Nice day," she said. "How was the ..." She stopped, crinkled her nose and looked around curiously. Burt had nowhere to turn. No one else to blame. He felt the blood drain from his head, heart pounding like a kettle drum. He could scream aloud like Jim Carrey in *Liar Liar,* "It was me!" but he didn't.

Instead, she shrugged and said, "You know, I told those trash men to stop using the public elevators. I'll report this to the Manager."

Huh? "Right. Oh yes! Right, trash men." *What trash men?* "I agree. Those guys have no consideration!"

Folders in hand, Denise exited the 10th Floor, nodding, smiling, leaving Burt to deal with his personal trauma. When it all passed and Burt was back at his desk on the fourth floor, he took a long breath and pondered the moment. There were so many ways that woman could have handled it. She could have given him a dirty look. Or said something like...

"My God, man, did you blow a whopper fart or what?"

"Good lord, it stinks in here!"

"Argghh, I'm gonna throw up!"

"Mister, if you must pass gas, please do it outside an elevator."

"Disgusting!"

She knew there had been no garbage men. She could have made him feel lower than a worm. Yet, she chose to be the consummate actress, with kindness and understanding. Any other choice would have been humiliating.

He pictured that gorgeous woman somehow differently now, not as some hot chick to gawk at, but as a human being with a thoughtful brain and a compassionate heart. This may have been an insignificant blip in the life of two people, but somehow it would always be remembered.

Cool lady, that secretary.

The Funeral

"What's the use of being loved, if the loved doesn't know it?"
— Anon

"Thank you all for coming here today. My father would have been so pleased to know that he had so many friends who cared so much. I also want to thank the Riverside Memorial Center for their generosity in providing this beautiful chapel for the PBA."

Victoria Vizzini-Morgan stood proud and composed at the podium as she began a brief but poignant tribute to her father. Easels of flowers framed the stage on all sides, along with enlarged lifetime photographs of Frank Vizzini, thin then portly, young then old, with a mane of black hair and then a few strands to cover the bald. They also showed his family members including his beloved daughter from when she was a baby. Above, on a seven-foot screen, an on-going slide show depicting the life of Frank Vizzini most people knew little about.

"I only wish my mother could also have been here to see the outpouring of love that people had for my father. Sadly, she passed away just four months ago, the day before we found out that my father had pancreatic cancer. She never knew. Thank God."

Over one hundred friends and associates were seated in

pews, old and young, black and white, men and women, some weeping, some somber. Victoria continued. "As most of you know, my father not only was a thirty-four year veteran of the Miami-Dade Police Department, he was active in youth sports. His coaching in baseball and football helped many deprived youngsters to receive scholarships into college. He also wrote numerous articles for police magazines, providing up-to-date information about the latest in firearms technology. During his stellar career, he saved many lives, and despite the fact that he took bullet wounds on three occasions, he was always proud to say he never had to shoot anyone in his life. During his last eight years on the job, he gave ten percent of his salary to Boys Town." She stopped a moment and panned the audience with gentle smile. "Well, enough from me. It was my father's last wish that we do not engage in a weepy cry-fest, but celebrate the goodness of his life and all that he did for others. He did not want a religious service because he felt religion was a private matter, not to be imposed on everyone else. So, we'll dispense with that. Anyone who wishes to pray for my father is certainly welcome to do so during a moment of meditation. Please honor the silence for one minute."

The chapel fell silent for sixty seconds as the slide show continued to play on the screen above.

"Thank you. My father asked we have a joyous service that will pay tribute to his life, as remembered by several of his friends and comrades. He specifically asked that the congregation hear from four people of his choosing. Then, if anyone else wishes to speak, please feel free." She raised her arm in gesture to a heavy-set fellow in the first pew. "First, we'll hear from Harry McGuire. Please, Harry."

Grey and riddled with arthritis, in his late sixties, big Harry used a cane to help himself to the podium.

"I knew Frank since we went to the academy together in 1974." Harry choked up, used a handkerchief, then continued. "Excuse me, please. This was the greatest man I ever knew. We worked on the road together, shared drinks, parties, and even funerals. He was at every christening for my three babies. I loved that man. I only wish I had stayed closer in touch after we retired. Good-bye, Frank."

Victoria then called upon Chief Barbara McGill Davis, head of the Police Operations Division. Dressed in dark business attire, Barbara had been sitting toward the rear of the room which required a slow walk in black stilettos to the podium. Now in her late fifties, her poise and good looks still turned heads among the male lookers. Neat, organized, stoic, she took the microphone. "I loved Frank Vizzini. He was the first male cop that accepted me in the crime scene unit back in '78. And, what a looker he was. He took time and showed me everything about crime scenes, but he never came on to me like most other chauvinist cops. To my disappointment, I might add. Frank devoted his life to helping others. He was the greatest cop I ever knew."

Victoria then called upon Billie Mangelino, star outfielder for the Miami Marlins.

In his mid-twenties, tanned and with movie-star good looks, clad in an Italian suit, William Mangelino started to speak, then caught himself tearing up. "I'm sorry," he said. "Give me a moment." He gritted and grimaced, then composed his demeanor at the podium. "I don't know what my life would have been if it were not for Frank Vizzini. Probably, buying and selling drugs in the streets of Miami. I came from a children's home, my parents died when I was a kid. No one gave a damn for me, except for Frank Vizzini. He saw my potential, and he developed it, spending days and nights on his time off, playing ball, making contacts with big names. I loved that man. I only wish I had stayed closer in touch. I never thought anything would bring him down. Good-bye Frank. Thanks for everything."

Victoria thanked Billie Mangelino, then called upon the Police Director himself, Eduardo Valenzuela. Not everyone knew the new boss personally. With only fifteen years in law enforcement, Valenzuela promoted rapidly through the ranks. Later, the former Director, Alfred Stoscko, was fired and then indicted on charges of corruption. The opening for a new director was ripe for an Hispanic and Valenzuela was right for the job.

Tall and handsome, with an engaging smile, the Cuban-American took the podium. "Hello everyone. I don't know why Mr. Vizzini would have wanted me to say anything. I know he was a respected man. In my early career, we worked in Homicide at the same time, though we were never partners. I hardly knew him. He took over a crime scene investigation from me one time, because I had to go to court. He got good evaluations. He was always very polite and respectful in my presence. My condolences to his daughter."

After that flat tribute, Victoria asked if anyone else would like to offer a few words. One hand shot upward from the center of the room. A young woman, about forty, stocky, short black hair, smartly dressed in a black suit, stood and walked to the podium. Victoria was taken aback, not knowing who she was.

"Hello. My name is Leah Tannenbaum." The woman panned the room a moment as she paused. Then came the shocker. "Frank Vizzini was my father."

The audience erupted into a flurry of buzz. Victoria dropped her jaw.

"All my life, I knew that Herb Tannebaum was not my real father, but my mother continued to lie to me, because she was embarrassed that she had conceived a child out of wedlock while she was engaged to someone else. When I found out the truth fifteen years ago, I met with Frank Vizzini and asked him. He said, 'Yes. I'm your biological father.' He owned up to it and offered to help me with anything I wanted. I didn't need anything, because my family is well off. But I did need validation, and if it were possible, even a little bit of love. Though his wife or his daughter..." Leah then peered lovingly into Victoria's eyes. "...knew anything about me, I asked him to let it stay that way. I didn't want to cause a wedge between the woman he loved and the daughter he cherished. But he continued to write me letters and to visit me in St. Augustine whenever he had the chance. I got to know my biological father. I feel privileged and honored to stand here today, and offer my love to Victoria as a sister she never knew. As for Frank Vizzini, he was a class act. I loved him very much."

Victoria sat stunned. The entire affair had been carefully staged and controlled, just the way her father wanted. She hadn't expected this. Yet, a feeling of goodness came over her like a warm hug from a loved one. At first she felt resentment for never being told. But she knew her father well, and could imagine that he would have honored her wishes in that way. Without hesitation, she approached Leah as she stepped from the podium. They embraced strongly like they would never let go, while the tears flowed and the hearts billowed. "We'll talk more later, okay?" Victoria said.

"Yes."

It took a few moments for Victoria to compose herself. Then, "Well, wasn't that a surprise? Whew. Okay, we have another surprise for you. A month ago, my father asked me to get him a video camera. I didn't know why, until recently. He asked me to share a few of his solitary moments with you all, from his bedroom. When the video is over, please don't leave. There is a procession that will follow."

Victoria pushed the buttons and got the video rolling on the large screen monitor at the front of the chapel. Sure enough, a thin, gaunt Frank Vizzini in his robe, sitting in a comfy chair, was looking straight into the camera with his trademark Italian smile.

"Hi everyone. Glad you're here. Ya know, I wanted this to be a celebration of joy, not sorrow, cause I had a great friggin' life! Sure, I woulda liked to have stuck it out longer, but ya know, I missed out on nothin'. I had the wife of anyone's dreams, a woman from heaven who I didn't deserve. And we had what I could only describe as the perfect daughter. Despite all my faults and crazy antics, including a few years of letting booze get the best of me, Victoria and Margaret only had forgiveness in their hearts. No man could have loved anyone more than I loved my wife and my daughter.

"I got a few things I wanna say. First, to you Harry McGuire. Big Mac. Remember all those good times together? We made a helluva pair, didn't we? I know you're gonna say nice things at my service. So let me say the same...I love you too. Okay, man? I love you, okay? That says it all.

"Now, you, Barbara. Uh, I mean, Chief Davis. I'm real proud a you, what you did, moving up like that. Cause you're really smart. More important, you're honest. Too bad that ain't what you're gonna be best remembered for, and you know it." The audience began to chuckle. "You gotta be the hottest female division chief in history. You certainly were the hottest cop I ever worked with. If I wasn't such a happily married man, I woulda hit on you like a stick to a drum. Man. But it never went to your head. Love ya, kid. And you know what I mean.

"Billie Mangelino. What a kid. My pride and joy. The son I never had. I'm a proud coach, a proud cop and a proud surrogate step-father. You're goin' to the Hall of Fame one day. I only wish I had your money. Geez, contracts for five million a year? But you gotta learn one thing, Billie. Never lose sight of your roots, just because you hit the big time. I haven't heard from you in three years. That's my only disappointment. But, I understand, you're young and all caught up in yourself. It's okay. And I know you love me. Cause I love you, kid.

"Eddie Valenzuela. Oh, excuse me. I mean, Director Eduardo Valenzuela. I want to thank you for attending this affair and for whatever remarks you have to offer. I gotta be honest. I wanted you at the services out of respect for your position. But I suspect you're going to say something like you hardly knew me, and can't think of much to say. So, let me remind you. When you were in uniform, I saw how sharp you were on a crime scene and I read some of your reports. They were some of the best by a uniformed rookie. You were an obscure cop then. No one knew who you were, but I knew you would be a great homicide detective. It was me who went to bat for you to the captain and the chief of detectives, against some tough opposition I might add, and got them to bring you in. Sure enough, you shined, like I knew you would, and before long, everyone in the political arena knew Eduardo Valenzuela. I helped you rise into the spotlight. You never acknowledged that, you never thanked me. A few years later, after you promoted up, I asked for a little favor, to help out another employee. You turned me down. In the presence of others you pretended like I was a peon working under the king. But, you know something, you validated my eye for talent, just like I knew Billie Mangelino would make it big, I knew you would too. You're welcome. And thanks for the inspiring words. But, you still gotta lot to learn.

"Okay, a few more people I wanna address. I suspect some of my friends will be too shy to speak at the podium, so let me point you out.

"Douglas Stivic, we were tight once. Don't know what happened. It's like we were never friends. It's part my fault. Must be five years since we talked. But, you were there for me in the old days when it counted. I love you, man.

155

"Willie Sampson. Hope you're here. You were treated like crap by the homicide guys in '77. I know it must have been tough, being one of two blacks in an all-white unit. But you overcame prejudice and adversity, and eventually made it to the rank of major. It was a privilege working under you in uniform and in Detective Division. Sorry I never told you that. You served with honor and dignity.

"Marion Uhr. You were a great secretary, but when you wanted to become a cop, I tried to talk you out of it. You were so damn small and fragile, I thought. I didn't think you could cut the mustard. But you proved me wrong. Two-gun Marion, they called you, after three shoot-outs, all of 'em ending in the bad guys getting whacked and you blowing smoke from the muzzle of your piece. When we worked together in homicide, you were the best female interrogator I ever saw. Don't know if anyone ever told you that. Boy, you had a way of locking a killer's heart in the palm of your hand. But more than anything, you were a great mom and loving wife to Bernie. I was so happy that you beat breast cancer. Love ya, kid.

"I just gotta add one more thing. To those I hurt in — my early days, I'm sorry. I'm really sorry. I wish I could take it all back. You know who you are.

"And listen. Don't cry cause of me. Dyin' is part of living. Everyone has their turn. Now it's my turn. What's the big friggin deal?

"Okay, that's it folks. I could ramble on and on, but it's time for a little music. Keep on enjoying every minute of life while you can. See ya on the next shift. Victoria, take it away."

As the monitor screen dimmed to dark, Frank Vizzini's daughter stood at the podium one more time and invited Leah to come up and join her as her newfound sister. With a broad smile and joy in her eyes, she leaned into the mike, "Ladies and gentlemen, I now present to you, the honor guard."

The eerie sounds of bagpipes began playing from the lobby outside the chapel. As the rear door opened, people turned their heads and shoulders as the gentleman piper, dressed in tartan plaid and an Irish tam, stepped through and stood at the rear of the center aisle, playing continuously. Behind him, a police honor guard consisting of three decorated officers in formal uniforms held the flag of the United States and the flag of the State of Florida, while the other shouldered a rifle. They stood at attention waiting for the piper to begin his march down the aisle. Many people in the audience held handkerchiefs to their eyes as the procession continued on. The strains of *Auld Lang Syne* rang through the chapel.

Folks stirred and looked up, down and around. From behind the honor guard, as the march began, a wheelchair followed pushed by a tall man in a black suit. As the wheelchair reached the center aisle and began rolling forward, the audience gasped in chorus. Several people stood up. One man shouted, "Oh My God." Another, "Jesus, Lord!" Another, "What?" Another, "You gotta be kidding...I don't believe it." Another, "Holy shit!"

Attendees bawled aloud as they watched a ghostly but defiant Frank Vizzini raise one hand above his head, bearing the hint of a smile while the chair rolled down the aisle.

Victoria felt the hair rise on her arms as the congregation went into a state of utter shock. Suddenly, Director Valenzuela bolted from the room and out the back door. Marion Uhr stepped from her pew and leaned over the chair being occupied by Frank Vizzini, as if she did not believe it was him. He patted her on the shoulder, and smiled. Willie Sampson and Big Mac came forward to touch him.

Victoria took the mike with tears rolling down her cheeks. "Ladies and gentlemen, I present my father, Frank Vizzini. He will explain. Please listen." She leaned over, kissed her father on the forehead, and handed him the mike.

Those who stood, sat down to listen. Many held handkerchiefs to their faces.

Covered with a blanket to his chest, the hunched, dying man in the wheelchair turned and faced the audience at floor level holding a wobbly mike close to his lips. Obviously sapped of strength, it presented a struggle but he was not to be denied this moment.

"A couple years ago, I did a eulogy for my best friend, Charlie Young." Frank paused to catch his breath. "I said glowing things. We all said glowing things. But what the frig good was it, if Charlie never heard them? Understand?" Gasping for breath, Frank paused again. The chapel remained silent. "Charlie never knew how much he was loved. And I was just as guilty, because I never told him that while he was alive. Remember that. I was too friggin shy. So, excuse me this little party. If you think I'm being selfish, well...I am. Your heartfelt words mean much more to me today, than after I'm dead. This was the only way. I'm sorry. Well, no. I ain't sorry. Thank you everyone. I love you too."

He turned to face the two women on the dais and motioned for them both to come forward. Victoria broke out in tears. "Why didn't you tell me?"

Leah stooped close to the chair as Frank lay his hand on her cheek while looking up to Victoria. "Don't ask. Just love her." he said. "I'm sorry for whatever I've done wrong. But I'll always love you. Both of you."

Several more friends came to offer, hands, hearts, hugs and kisses, including Barbara Davis, Marion Uhr and Billie Mangelino. The excitement sapped what little strength Frank Vizzini had left.

Finally, he motioned for Victoria to lean over in order to whisper into her ear, "Let's go, baby doll. The funeral is over. Now I gotta die."

About the Author

MARSHALL FRANK is a retired homicide detective and police captain from the Miami-Dade Police Department, in Miami, Florida where he served in many capacities including head of CSI. Also a former symphony violinist, he has authored thousands of published articles, plus ten books, including five suspense novels. He lives in Central Florida with his wife, Suzanne. Visit his web site at www.marshallfrank.com or contact him at MLF283@aol.com